# TAME THE PLAYER

HOPE FORD

Tame The Player © 2024 by Hope Ford

Editor: Kasi Alexander

Proofreader: Nicole Graf

Cover Photographer: CJC Photography

Cover Models:  Mitch & Amanda

Cover Design: Lori Jackson

Alternative Cover Design: Lori Jackson

All rights reserved.

1

## HOLDEN

I groan loudly into the empty room and then bury my face into the soft pillow. If I ignore the insistent knocking, maybe they'll go away.

As soon as the knocking ceases, I burrow myself deeper under the covers, drawing them over my head. I shut my eyes tight, hoping to fall back asleep, but my brain won't stop working. All I can think about is the game that's being played right now, and I'm not there… I won't even be donning the uniform.

It doesn't take much for me to imagine the feeling of being in that stadium with thousands of people cheering, and my teammates and I just trying to get a win. There's no other feeling like it.

Now the team is going to have to do it without me.

I'm debating on getting up and watching the game on television when I hear footsteps coming down the hall. Fuck me, I should have known that one of them would find the key that I gave them to my house. I should've reclaimed them a while back.

"Holden Gray, get your ass out here."

Growing up, when I would hear King holler my name that way, I would have come running. He may only be two years older than me, but he was like a dad to all of us. You didn't ignore King when he commanded your attention. However, I know exactly why he's here. He's going to tell me to get my shit together, and I'm not ready to hear it just yet.

My brothers Dom and Gabe decide to put their two cents in and state the obvious.

"He's in bed."

"Damn, this place is a disaster."

Yeah, I'm in bed, and the place is a disaster. My brothers are a couple of geniuses.

My sister, who is always the peacemaker and the only one that can get away with telling any of us what to do, comes into my room. "All right, guys, leave him be. Go on and get started cleaning up the living room, turn the game on, and Holden will be out in just a minute."

I don't even have to see her and I know she's waving the boys out of the room and looking at me with that pensive, worried look she has. My brothers won't deny her. Chrissy is the youngest of all of us, and we've always looked out for her. But today it seems she's determined to look out for me. As soon as the others are gone, I can feel the dip on the bed where she sits down. "Bub, it's okay. It's a strain, that's all."

I would much rather lie here and wallow in my own self-pity, but I can't just ignore Chrissy. After taking a deep breath, I force myself to unwrap from my cover cocoon and sit up. Stretching my arms out, ignoring the pain on my shoulder, I smile at her. "I'm getting up."

She measures me with a look, and I hate seeing pity on her face. Chrissy is the only one that can get away with it. She's biting her lip and looking at me nervously, letting me know something is up. She could never hide things from us. "Spill it. What's going on in that pretty head of yours?"

"I looked at your MRI. There's no tear, Holden. It's a strain."

She's not telling me anything that I don't

already know, but I do appreciate the fact she's a nurse and trying to reassure me. I stand up and grab my shirt off the back of the chair and pull it over my head. "I know, rotator cuff strain, but my coach still benched me."

She crosses her arms over her chest and eyes me warily. She knows how I am. Hell, my brothers and I are all stubborn, and poor Chrissy has to deal with it all the time. "The keyword here is strain, Holden. Think about it. You do a few months of physical therapy and then you'll get back on the field."

*Knock. Knock.* My brother Gabe is leaning against the opened door of my room, and he stares between Chrissy and me, swinging his head back and forth. "Hey, what's going on in here?"

Chrissy huffs and stands up. "We're just talking, Gabe. If you're here to give him crap, he doesn't need it."

I watch as Gabe and Chrissy square off.

"I didn't come in here to give him crap."

"No, you came in here to be nosy."

Gabe is taller than all of us, but he stands to his full height and glares at me. "No, I'm wondering what you're doing in the bedroom with my brother."

Automatically, my hand goes to my stomach

because I'm sure I'm going to be sick. "She's our sister, Gabe."

He glares at Chrissy, who has her hands on her hips and is standing toe to toe with him. Gabe's nostrils flare, and I realize that he's really pissed off. "Not really."

I position myself between them. I'm not sure what's been going on between the two of them lately, but it's something. Gabe is my blood brother. Chrissy is our foster sister, and Ledger, Gabe, and Dom are our foster brothers, but we were all raised in the same foster home most of our young life. To me, they are my family. Exhausted, I put an arm around Chrissy's shoulder and push her through the door while Gabe steps to the side. "Hey you two, no fighting. This is supposed to be about me and my career falling apart, remember?"

And just like that, Chrissy is giving me the pity look again. "Your career is not falling apart. It's a rotator cuff strain. You take care of it and you'll be back at it."

I give my sister a hug and then walk into the living room and spot my new sister-in-law. "How's it going, Haven?"

I lean over and kiss her on the top of the head

as my brother and Haven's husband, King, growls at me. "Watch it, Gray."

I sit down in my chair, and even though I've tried to tune out the ballgame on the television since I walked into the room, I'm drawn to it and see that my team, the Jasper Bears, are down three to one in the bottom of the 6th.

Dom grabs a piece of pizza from the box on the coffee table. "Don't worry, brother. There's still plenty of game to be played."

Gabe sits across the room, not even in a position to watch the television. I guess he's not here for the game. "So what's the doctor's saying? What's the plan?"

"Physical therapy."

Dom chugs his beer. "Well, do the therapy and then get back to work."

Chrissy puts a plate in Gabe's hands. He takes it, and they exchange words before she turns to me and piles a plate with pizza and puts it in my lap. "Eat up. I'm working on a therapist that will come here. I already have one in mind, but it's going to cost you. She's the best at Jasper Hospital."

I could argue with her, but I know it won't do any good. I want a few more days of wallowing in my self-pity, but I've had trouble finding a therapist with the availability I need for the next two months. "I need to be back in the game in two months. I have to make it to the playoffs."

Chrissy gives me an encouraging smile. "And you can do it… if you have an in-house therapist."

I almost choke on the piece of pizza I'm eating. I'll grant it to her, my house is big. It has everything I need to get back into the game. It has a workout room with every workout machine I would need. A therapy room with top of the line everything. This house has four guest rooms, so technically someone could stay here and I wouldn't even have to see them outside of therapy, but the idea of having someone here all the time just doesn't sit well with me. I like my privacy. "No. I can drive to therapy."

Chrissy rolls her eyes. "You're going to drive into Jasper every day for therapy? Sure, that makes a lot of sense."

Gabe points at Chrissy and nods at me. "I agree. You need someone in house. You don't want to traipse through town for every appointment. If they're here, they can help you with your workouts and everything… maybe even help you heal faster."

I hold my hands up. I know if I say no, they're just going to keep arguing their case, so I do what I have to do to get them off my back. I know they're just trying to help, but I'm not in the mood for it right now. I'm still trying to wallow if only they'd let me. "I'll think about it."

Chrissy claps her hands together. "Okay, I'll get on it."

King goes over to where Haven's sitting. He pulls her up and then sits down, pulling her into his lap. He kisses his wife and wraps his arms around her. We're all watching them, and I see the same look on my brothers' and sister's face as I'm sure is on mine. Since King met and married Haven, it's brought a different level to our family dynamic. It's nice seeing that at least one of us was able to find love.

King whispers something to Haven and then clears his throat when he notices us all watching them. "So the playoffs are in two months. Can the Bears get there without you?"

I'm not arrogant, but I know what I bring to the team. If you look at stats and everything on paper, the chances are slim. Not only am I considered the number one catcher in the league but I'm also the third in the league for home runs. There's no doubt that they are going to hurt without me there, but I have faith in my team. I have to, there's no other option. "Yeah, they'll get us there. And come hell or high water, I'm going to be back for the playoffs."

We watch a little of the game, and when we get to the middle of the eighth and it's tied four to four, I drop the bombshell that I can't stop thinking about. "So the main question I've been asked is if I'm going to retire at the end of this season."

I'm not sure what I expected, but it wasn't this. Every one of them stares back at me, and none of them seem surprised by my statement. It's almost as if they've thought about it themselves. I jam my hand through my hair and stare at the television. "I mean, I'm thirty-eight years old. I guess it's a given that people would wonder, and it seems my body is giving out on me."

"Bullshit," King practically bellows, and Haven jerks in his lap.

He apologizes to her and then turns back to me. "Seriously, Holden. That's bullshit, and you know it. You're not going to retire until you're ready. You're not going to let some lame asshole make you think now's the time. You're going to get your arm better, win the playoffs, and then you decide what you're going to do. It's your life, you live it the way you want."

My whole body heats as emotion rolls through

me. My heart is racing, and there's a tremble in my hands, but I nod at my big brother. He's the man that worked his ass off to get me to the big leagues. He's the reason I was able to get trained by some of the country's best athletes. He made it possible for me to get where I am now, and I know he's right. I'll retire when I think I'm ready.

I lean forward, resting my elbows on my knees. The time for self-pity is over. A new determination has come over me, and I'm going to prove to everyone that I still have plenty of game left in me. "Thanks, King."

He nods at the same time Dom jumps from his seat with a loud holler. "Yes, go ball! Go ball!"

All eyes turn to the screen in front of us, and everyone in the living room starts punching their fists in the air. The Bears did it. They won a game against a team that was favored to win. There are plenty of more games to play, but if my team can get us there, I'll be back for the playoffs.

2

––––––––––

CATHERINE

The sound of chairs scraping across the floor and people talking fills the room as I try to eat my lunch. My friend Bethany, a nurse here at the hospital, is telling me some gory story from her morning working in the emergency room, and suddenly I'm not that hungry anymore. I point with my fork at my plate. "Really? I'm eating here."

She just laughs and waves me off. "You're so sensitive, Catherine. I didn't even go into detail."

I lean forward. "You said—and I quote—'he was cut wide open, and his intestines were hanging out. I had to shove them back in and just hold them there until the doctor got there.' That's quite a bit of detail… and I'm eating spaghetti, no less."

Bethany just laughs again. "Fine. I'm done. What about you? How was your morning?"

Since I can no longer stomach the noodles, I move them around on my plate. "Well, let's see, Cole had workouts this morning and had to be at the school gym at six, so I dropped him off."

Bethany holds her hands up. "Wait. He has workouts before school? He's thirteen."

I snort because I think I said the same thing when Cole told me he was going to start having two practices a day. "Yeah, they're called two-a-days. They do weights in the morning before school and then after school, they have baseball practice…. Anyway, so I dropped him off and met Jeremy for breakfast—"

Bethany starts hopping up and down in her seat and wiggling her eyebrows at me. "Ooooh, yeah, get to the good part. Did he jelly your toast? Put syrup on your—"

"Shhhh!" I whisper to her. "Geez, Bethany, really?"

She sits up a little straighter and doesn't even try to hide the disappointment on her face. "You're right. I've met Jeremy. I don't even need to ask because I know he didn't do anything to your lady bits."

I push my plate away and pick up my water instead. "We've only been dating two months."

"Two months, seven dates, and you've kissed. You have to be the most boring couple—"

Thankfully, Bethany stops talking when our friend Chrissy sets her tray down next to us. She sits down with a look at Bethany. "I hear you had your hands in guts this morning."

"Geez, you two should come with a warning label. Can't we just have a normal lunch without talking about internal organs and all that?"

Chrissy and Bethany both laugh, and I know they do it because they think it's hilarious that I can't stomach their job. Yeah, even though I once wanted to be a nurse, it was smart of me to go the physical therapy direction instead. I may have to deal with some gross feet sometimes, but at least I don't have to worry about organs falling out of bodies.

Chrissy looks remorseful. "You're right, Catherine. That was wrong of me, especially since I know you have a sensitive stomach." She looks down at my plate. "Uh, spaghetti probably wasn't the best choice for today."

I'm about to grab my tray and leave when

Chrissy stops me. "I'm sorry, okay? Seriously, though, I need to talk to you about something."

I can only imagine what's about to come out of her mouth. "What do you need to talk to me about? And please, don't make it gory."

Chrissy nods, and with a serious expression, she pulls out a file that was under her tray. "I need a favor, and I know when I say it, you're going to say no, but I need you to hear me out."

Intrigued, I look between her and the file she's gripping tightly in her hands. I can't read the name on it from where I'm sitting. "Tell me about this favor."

Her eyes light up with hope. "Okay, it's my brother, Holden, the baseball player. He has a rotator cuff strain, and he needs a physical therapist for the next two months."

I'm not sure what the problem is. "Well, have him make an appointment. You know the hospital will fit him in."

She points at me. "But I want you… I want him to be seen by you."

"Chrissy, you're an employee, they'd pull strings for you. Plus, he's a professional baseball player. The hospital will eat it up and love the publicity around it."

She fidgets in her seat and scrunches her nose up. "That's the thing. In order for him to get back in the game in two months, the therapy will need to be intense. We need someone that can come to him." Before I can object, she holds her hand up. "His house has everything you'd need. He has a whole weight room, therapy table, bands, ice bath, hot tub, the works."

I can see how desperate she feels about this. I've known Chrissy for a little over a year now, and even though I don't know her whole story, I do know that she loves her foster brothers and would do anything for them. "Look, I get it, I do. But I have a case load right now, and there's no way I can do it and drive back and forth to—where does he live?"

"Whiskey Run. He lives in Whiskey Run."

I'm startled because I live in Whiskey Run and had no idea that Holden Gray from the Jasper Bears lives there. If Cole knew, he'd flip. Heck, he'd also flip if he knew I was turning down an opportunity to heal one of his favorite big league players. "Right, I can't drive back and forth to Whiskey Run."

Chrissy's face is set in determination. "But that's the thing, you wouldn't have to drive back and forth. You could stay with him. He has four guestrooms."

I sit back in my seat, and my mouth drops. If she was making this offer to any of my colleagues, they would drop everything to do it. I mean, what woman is going to say no to staying at the home of the Holden Gray? Ugh, me, that's who. "I can't stay at his house. I have Cole… and Jeremy."

Bethany lets out a snort. "Yeah, like Jeremy's going to care. He's gotta put some work in before he can have a say in where you spend your time, Catherine."

I stick my tongue out at her. It's not very ladylike, but it's all I've got. It's not like I can flip her off in the middle of the cafeteria. But the sentiment is the same because I know she's right. Quite honestly, Jeremy probably wouldn't care if I stayed at Holden Gray's house. He would find some way to compute the overtime and how it's good for my business or something.

I hold both hands up in front of the two women that are looking at me expectantly. "I'm not staying at Holden Gray's house."

"But—" Chrissy starts, and I shut it down real quick.

"Nope, it's not happening. I cannot stay at his house."

Chrissy deflates a little, but she's not giving up. "Okay, fine. Well, you live in Whiskey Run, too, right? You would be close anyway, so surely we can work something out."

I'm about to say no. She has to see it, and she leans over and wraps her hand around mine. "Please, Catherine. Baseball is his whole life, and I've never seen him like this. You can help him, I know you can."

Bethany's looking at me like she already knows what I'm going to say. Chrissy is giving me the most pleading look, and I'm pretty sure she's going to cry if I say no. The truth is, I don't want to say no. I feel stuck lately, and maybe this is what I need. It would be a challenge, for sure, but I could do it. "Let me see his file."

Chrissy thrusts it at me, and Bethany stands up and pats Chrissy on the back. "Smart woman. If she looks at the file, there's no way she'll say no. I'm heading back, ladies. See you later."

"Bye," I mumble as I flip through the pages of Holden Gray's file. I can do this. I can help him. I close the file. "I'll see what I can do."

"Yes!" Chrissy yells, pumping her arm in the air.

She jumps up and comes around to hug me. As she squeezes the life out of me, I try to not get her hopes up even higher. "Stop. I said I'd see what I can do. I have to talk to the hospital and get it approved by them, and then I'd have to move my workload. I would like to meet him and get a feel of him and his attitude. There's a lot of moving parts here, and we'll just have to see what happens."

She pulls away and sits down in the chair next to me. Her whole body shudders as she takes a deep breath and lets it out. "I know it's a lot to ask, Catherine, but you're the best, and Holden… well, let's just say that he's a hard case. He's having a hard time with it all, and he feels like his career is up in the air… it's just…"

I pick up the file and tuck it under my arm. "I get it, Chrissy. I know… I promise, I'll do my best… okay?" I pick up my tray. "I'll call you this afternoon."

She's holding her hands together in front of her, and she doesn't have to tell me how much this means to her. I can see it on her face.

As I'm walking back to my office, I think about everything I know about Holden Gray. Not a lot in the grand scheme of things. I know he's one of Cole's favorite players, and I know he's one of Chrissy's foster brothers. I can imagine what it means to him to be injured and unable to play. This isn't a hobby for him; this is his career. The pressure has to be immense, and like I told Chrissy, I'm going to do what I can. I just need to convince the hospital to take this on.

## 3

## HOLDEN

I'm sitting across from Catherine and should be focusing on what she says instead of the way her lips are big, puffy, and pink, as if they're begging to be kissed. She's talking, using her hands as she tells me about the plan she's come up with, and all I can process is the fact that this is going to be my physical therapist and I'm going to be spending a lot of time with her. Now the whole idea Chrissy had about the therapist living here is sounding better and better.

"Mr. Gray… what do you think?"

All I can do is stare at her and try to form a sentence. "Sorry, what?"

She smirks at me, and I'm not sure if she realizes that I'm attracted to her or what, but she has to be used to getting reactions like mine from men. Catherine Maples is the most beautiful woman I've ever laid eyes on. Her blond hair is in a high ponytail, and her clear blue eyes are looking at me like she can see into my soul. She showed up in a pair of black pants and a polo shirt with the hospital's logo on her chest, but the plain uniform does nothing to hide the luscious curves of her body.

She lays the open file on the table between us. "Look, I know this is hard, Mr. Gray."

"Holden," I tell her, wanting to hear her say my name.

"Holden," she repeats softly and then puts her palm flat on the file. "I know this is hard for you, but I think it's doable." She looks around the room. "Do you have somewhere that I can do an evaluation before we get too far into it?"

I shove my chair back and stand up. I'm not sure how I'm going to do with this woman's hands on me. "Sure, I have a therapy room next to the weight room."

That seems to perk her up. "You have a therapy room?"

I grumble because how else can I explain it? "Yeah, when you're a thirty-eight-year-old professional catcher who's played for as long as I have, you need help more days than not."

She leaves the file on the table and follows behind me. We go to the basement, and I show her the gym and then take her to the therapy room. I point out everything I have. "If there's anything else you'd need, I can get it."

She looks around the room in awe. "It looks to me that you have everything we could possibly need." She points to the place in front of her. "Stand here."

I move and stop in front of her. She's smaller than me, and it's obvious we would fit together perfectly. She takes a step back. "Can you touch your toes?"

"It's my arm that is hurt."

She crosses her arms over her chest and smiles at me. "It's your shoulder that is hurt, but I also know that if we focus on your shoulder, it's going to leave other parts of your body vulnerable. You're an elite athlete, Holden. If I do this, I will be treating your whole body."

I suck in a breath because just the idea of her putting her hands on me puts me on edge. *You've been celibate for too long, Gray.*

I take too long to answer.

She repeats the question. "Can you touch your toes?"

I lean forward and put my hands flat on the floor in front of me. As a catcher, I have to be pretty limber, and I stretch daily. I have to or else I'll end up injured for sure. Her hand goes to my back, and I raise up so quickly it's comical.

Worriedly, she asks, "Did you feel pain anywhere when you touch your toes?"

I hold in my groan because the only pain I feel right now is in my southern region, and I'm sure she's not talking about that. "Nope, no pain."

She walks me through a few exercises, and when she finally gets to my right arm, I school my expression. *I will not show pain. I will not show pain.* Whatever I gotta do to get back on the field, I'll do it. Even if it means sucking up any ounce of pain I feel.

She huffs out her breath. "Mr. Gray."

I give her a pointed look, and she relents. "Holden, if you want to be back by the playoffs, we have to be honest with each other. If you're in pain, I have to know it. You have to tell me where it hurts and when. Got it?"

I nod my head, and she starts moving my arm, watching my face closely. She's so close that I can smell her coconut shampoo. When my arm goes too far back, my forehead creasing is the only indication that I might be in pain. She holds my arm in place and then tilts her head to the side and just waits.

"Yeah, right there, I feel it."

She releases my arm and then takes a step back. "Your range of motion on that side is way less. I'm thinking it has something to do with your throwing technique, but I've watched the video of the play you made where you think you might have hurt it. It was a strenuous throw for your arm."

"I got him out running to second."

She laughs. "Yeah, you did. I want to get your arm healed and then get it healthy so that when you have to make plays like that, you can do it without injury."

"By the playoffs?"

She doesn't answer right away, and it's like I'm holding my breath waiting for her to tell me what I want to hear. Finally, she puts me out of my misery. "We can get you back by the playoffs, but there's going to be a lot of work involved. For an elite athlete, you have to focus on your nutrition, strength, and cardiovascular training for your whole body and intense therapy on your arm. You have to be focused and stay focused. You have to do what I tell you to do."

I hate when anyone tells me what to do, but something tells me it's going to be different with Catherine. "I can do it."

"Okay, and one more question."

Hell, I figure we're already over the hard part, so I give her an encouraging nod.

She searches my face for a second and then asks me the one question that I've been trying to avoid. "What's your long-term goal here?"

I can't hide my reaction. I've tried to tamp down all the thoughts of retiring. I've avoided all the sports channels so I don't have to hear everyone's thoughts on my career and how it's ending. "You think I need to retire?"

Shock registers on her face, and she holds her hand up. "First of all, you should know that I know nothing about professional baseball. My knowledge consists of thirteen-year-old baseball. So I'll ask you the same question you asked me. Do you think you need to retire?"

Instead of answering her, I start to pace across the room. I wasn't ready for the question she asked me, and I'm not sure how to answer it. I'm reaching the point where I want to retire—I'm ready for it, and before I was injured, I was considering it—but I don't want to go out like this. Stalling, I ask her, "Why do you know about thirteen-year-old baseball?"

"My son plays at the middle school here in Whiskey Run."

I stop pacing and zero in on her left hand. I look for a ring, and when I don't see one, the relief hits me fast and hard. "Your son?"

She nods. "Yeah, now quit avoiding the question and tell me… do you think you need to retire?"

I jut my chin at her, and she doesn't back down. Reluctantly, I tell her what I've been thinking. "Before my injury, I was thinking about this being my last season. I'm getting old—well, old for playing baseball and old for being a catcher. It has wrecked my body. But now, no, I'm not ready to retire. I don't want to end my career because of an injury. I want to end it on my own terms."

She doesn't laugh and doesn't even crack a smile. She gives me a firm nod and tells me the one thing I've been waiting to hear. "I can help you get back on the field, playing pain-free, by the playoffs."

## 4

## CATHERINE

I usually don't give hope to a patient like I am right now, but I think Holden Gray needs it. I help people every day, and it's not lost on me how important this is to him. Baseball is his whole life, and I can respect the fact he wants to retire on his own terms. I get that he doesn't want any regrets and all that.

He's taken aback by my statement, but there's no skepticism when he says, "Okay, so when can you move in and get started?"

We're too close. This room feels like it's closing in on me. "Do you care if we move back to the living room?"

Without question, he walks out of the room, and I follow behind him. I try to ready my speech on the way so that by the time we make it to the living room, I blurt out, "I live just fifteen minutes from here. I can come here for our appointments."

He crosses his arms over his chest. "The position is for a live-in physical therapist. And you said it would be a whole body regimen, so I'm assuming it would be every day. It makes sense that you would stay here."

"I can't do that."

"I will pay for the inconvenience, and of course you'd be paid for being here full-time."

I don't even have to think about it. "No."

His jaw tightens, and it's obvious that people don't usually tell him no. He doesn't like it. "Why?"

I point at a chair. "Can we sit down and talk about this?"

"Shit, yeah, I'm sorry. Sit down. Can I get you a drink or anything?"

I rest my hands on my knees. "No, I'm fine. Holden, I can't stay here because like I told you, I have a thirteen-year-old son."

He gestures to the ceiling. "I should have shown you around. I have four guestrooms. You and your son could each have a room here."

I hesitate but only because I'm trying to think of

another tactic. For a high-profile client like this, it makes sense to have a live-in therapist. It's been done before, so it's not out of the ordinary or anything, and heck, Cole would love the idea of staying here with his idol, but I can't give in. I need to keep everything as professional as I can. Holden Gray has the reputation of being a charmer, and he's very handsome. It's a given that I'm attracted to him because who wouldn't be? And it's not like I don't trust myself because I know I can be professional, but why even put myself in this position? Nope, it doesn't matter if it's more convenient, I need to keep my distance.

He's smiling, and I have to look away because somehow he's even better looking when he smiles. "You're considering it."

"No."

He sits down on the coffee table in front of me. "Why not?"

"I'm not uprooting my son for two months."

He holds up one finger and starts counting off. "One, I can help your son with technique while you're here. Two, I would take care of room, board, regular twenty-four-hour pay, and a twenty thousand dollar bonus."

I start to panic. It's the deal of a lifetime, and

my son would die if he knew I was turning this down. "No."

"Thirty thousand dollars."

He's talking nonsense now. "What? Why? If you're ready to pay that kind of money, then you can hire a sports therapist. Someone that works regularly with professional athletes."

"I want you."

It's like a jolt to my system. Why does my heart do a little flip in my chest? "I uh… why?"

He leans forward, and our knees are almost touching. "Well, let's see. Why would I want you to be in charge of my therapy? You performed hand therapy on Doctor Trent when he had tendons cut in his hand in a car accident. He's the top heart surgeon in the South, and he trusted you with his hands. He's been back at work for three years and has saved countless lives since then."

My mouth drops, but he's not done yet. "You were in charge of the therapy for Josh Chambers, the running back for the Jasper Eagles."

I can't hold back my shock on this one. "That was all done on the down-low. No one was supposed to know about that."

"Josh told me about it and said you saved his career. I want the best, Catherine, and that's you. I want to play again, and I see the passion on your face when you talk about your job and what you can do. I want to do this with you."

*Say no. Say no.* That's what I'm repeating in my head, but I can feel myself giving in. "I would have to talk to my son first. I can't make this kind of decision without talking to him."

He nods his head, and by the look on his face, he thinks it's a done deal. He knows my son is going to be over the moon with us staying here, so I do what I think I need to do and tack on, "And my boyfriend. I'll need to see what he thinks about all this."

He tenses. "You have a boyfriend? I mean, of course you have a boyfriend. Who is it?"

I scoot back in my seat because it's intoxicating being this close to him. I need to say no, and that's the plan, but first I need to get out of here. I jump out of my seat and start walking out of the room. It's rude and unprofessional, but I can say the same about sitting here talking about my personal life as well.

He's hot on my heels, and I grab my file and make it to the front door. "So I'm going to talk to Cole and to Jeremy—"

He interrupts me. "Which is your son?"

"Cole. My son's name is Cole. I'll let you know something in a few days."

He opens the front door but stands partly in front of me. I ignore the way his shirt is tight across his muscled chest. I look away at the forearm that's blocking my way. His voice is gruff. "So talk to Cole and Jeremy but just know, Cat, I don't plan on taking no as an answer."

My breath hisses. "Cat?"

He licks his lips and nods his head. "Yeah, I think Cat suits you."

I pull at my shirt that suddenly feels too tight. "My name is Catherine."

He brings down his arm and crosses it over his chest. "I'll talk to you soon, Cat."

I open my mouth to say my full name again, but seeing the smirk on his face has me holding the file close to my chest, muttering bye, and walking past him. When I get to my car, I feel like I have to catch my breath. I don't even give myself a second to think back on the last hour I've spent with Holden Gray and his intense brown eyes, charm, and vulnerability. If I'm going to be able to help him, I'm going to have to keep it professional.

## 5

## HOLDEN

It's been two days, and I'm about to track Catherine Maples down. I gotta stop thinking about her and start focusing on staying fit and getting back in the game. Baseball has always been my priority, but there's been a shift in me since I met Cat two days ago. I swear at random times, I've smelled coconuts in my house, but I know it's crazy because there's no way she's left her scent here after being here less than an hour.

She's had plenty of time to talk to her son and her boyfriend, and so I've convinced myself she's going to say no. Which means I'm going to have to track down my sister and then convince her to give me Cat's phone number, and then I'm going to have to make her an offer she can't refuse.

It's insane how I was totally against having someone stay at my place, and now I'm totally convinced it's the best option. It's like there is no other option. I want Cat—and her son—here.

I pull at the weighted band and spread my arms wide. Pain shoots into my shoulder, and I try to hold the move but then finally let it go. In frustration, I groan and bring my arms in. As soon as I do, the pain goes away, and I get more discouraged. I've tried to stay positive, but I can't help but wonder how in the world I'm going to get better in two months.

The doorbell ringing has me running up the stairs and to the front door. The fact it could be Cat has me stopping before I open it and trying to catch my breath and pull myself together. I've never been this crazy over a woman, especially one I just met, but there's no denying there is something special about Cat Maples. I open the door, and there's no hiding the disappointment from my face. "Kendall... what are you doing here?"

She breezes past me and looks around my foyer before turning back to me. "You could at least act like you're happy to see me."

I look at the woman that I've dated on and off

for the past few months. She was hinting that she wanted me to give her a ring until I was injured. Which in itself was crazy because we've never even had sex. She was my plus one for some events, but my schedule doesn't allow for a lot of dating. We haven't seen each other since I got benched, and honestly I'm surprised that she's showed up at my house now. I lean against the open door. "I guess I'm just wondering what you're doing here, that's all."

She's not fazed by my indifference. "Come on, Holden, don't be like that. I've been worried about you."

I blurt out a laugh and shake my head before shutting the front door. If she was worried about me, she would have shown up before now. Maybe even called me to check on me when she found out I was not going to be playing in the game last week. "What are you doing here, Kendall?"

She reaches for me, and I take a step back. She pouts, but I'm not falling for it this time. In the past, I would give in to what she wanted, but I'm half out of patience. "I was in the middle of something, and I need to get back to it, so whatever you're here to say, please just say it."

She fidgets, her hands in front of her. "I just wanted to see how you're doing… what are the doctors saying?"

My shoulders tense, and I don't want to have this conversation with her. "I have a rotator cuff strain. I have to do physical therapy."

Her eyes light up. "And then you'll be able to play again?"

I'm about to say yes but then reconsider. "Who knows, Kendall? I mean, that's the goal, right? I want to play, but no one really knows for sure what's going to happen."

She looks uneasy, and I can see the way she's considering everything. She shakes her head. "So I've been thinking…"

Her voice trails off, and I should probably offer for her to come in or to sit down, but I don't. I know that all Kendall cares about is status. It was fine these past few months because I knew exactly what it was, but there's no reason to carry on with the charade. It's time for this to be over. "Go ahead, what have you been thinking?"

She puts on a fake smile. "I think I should give you space to heal. I know you want to focus on"— she waves her hand to my shoulder—"you know… everything. I don't want to be the one to stand between you and getting back into the action."

I don't even hesitate. "I think that's a good idea. I have a lot of doctor appointments, therapy appointments, and everything else. I need to focus."

She nods and couldn't be more obvious. "Right, and when you're back on the team then we can catch back up."

I grit my teeth because I know that's not going to happen. "Right, well, I better get back to it."

She's completely clueless about everything. She doesn't realize that I'm on to her. I know she was only wanting to date me because I'm a pro baseball player, and now that my future with the team is in question, she's not interested. I'm not a fool, and I've dealt with plenty of women like her in the past. I go to the door and hold it open for her.

She walks toward it and stops in front of me. She presses her chest against mine, goes to her tiptoes, and tries to kiss me. I turn my head at the last second, and her lips go to my cheek. If she's surprised, she doesn't act like it. Her smile remains, and she gives me a wave and walks out the door. As soon as she gets outside, I shut the door and pull my phone from my pocket. My sister answers on the first ring. "Hey, bub, how's it going?"

She's got that worried tone in her voice again. "I'm good. I need Catherine's number."

She's silent and then softly answers. "I can't give you her number. Why didn't you ask her for it when she was there?"

I lean my head back against the wall and hold in my groan. I didn't get her number because I thought she would say yes. I dangled the carrot, offering her an obscene amount of money, so who would have thought she'd have to think about it? "Have you talked to her? Is she taking the job?"

Chrissy laughs. "You said you didn't want someone to move in and then you told her it was a requirement."

Fuck! I could give in, but I want her here with me. But if my requirement means she won't come, then I'm willing to give in. Before I can tell Chrissy that, she continues. "She's working on it. I'm pretty sure the hospital has approved all her clients to be moved to other caseloads, and the last I heard, she was going to work things out with her family and everything."

I interrupt her. "So you won't give me her number?"

She laughs out loud. "It's against the rules,

Holden. Look, if you don't hear from her tomorrow, I'll give her a call. It's a lot. She's having to move her schedule for the next two months, she's having to figure things out with her kid and her boyfriend. All these things to make this work, so you have to give her a few days."

I'm probably wasting my time, but I don't know when to shut up. "Have you met her boyfriend?"

The longer Chrissy is silent, the more I realize I've fucked up. I don't know why it's so important to me, but it is. Chrissy lets out a little gasp. "Holden Gray, are you for real right now? Do you like her?"

"What's not to like? She's smart, she's beautiful, caring, and passionate about her job. I offered her a lot of money, and she had to think about it when most people would say yes on the spot while telling me they care about more than just money."

"Awwwwww, Holden," she sings-songs. "That's so sweet... but I know Catherine, she is by the book. She's not going to take the job if she thinks you're interested in her."

I groan and push my hand through the scruff on my chin. Every part of me wants to tell Cat that I like her, but there are so many things going against us already. She's going to be my physical therapist, she has a son—this can't be a fling or something, and she has a boyfriend. Nope, even though I'm attracted to her, I need to keep focused. I can be professional. But just as fast as I think it, I know I'm lying because there's no resisting Cat Maples. "You know I could just call Cat at the hospital, right?"

"Bub, listen to me. Catherine is not like the other women you date. She's down to earth, her kid comes first, she's the best mom I've ever met. She doesn't do flings."

I put my hand to my chest. I try to laugh it off, but her words hit a little hard. "Really, is that what you think of me, sis? I'm not—"

"You haven't had a serious relationship that I know of. Every picture online of you has a different woman draped on your arm, so forgive me if I think you're up to no good. Look, you need to focus on your health and getting better. Then you can worry about finding you a date for your next big event."

"It's not like that…" I start to refuse but then trail off. Maybe I'm being ridiculous. I'm going all crazy over some woman I met for an hour. I need to chill the fuck out. Maybe it's all the time I have on my hands, or maybe I'm just not thinking straight. Whatever it is, I need to get my shit together. "You know what, you're right. I'm being crazy. I'll give her until tomorrow. If she can't do it, then I'll need to find someone else. Thanks for talking me down, Chrissy."

She stutters, and her voice raises an octave. "What? No. I'm not saying you need to give up or anything, and I'm not saying that Catherine wouldn't be lucky to be with you. I'm just saying don't play with her. If you like her, then be right with her. She has a son… just don't hurt her."

As soon as she says it, she groans. "Darn, I'm not saying you'll hurt her, you're a good guy, but—"

"Chrissy, stop. You don't have to keep tiptoeing around me. I got it. I know what you're saying. Now can you get back to being the bossy little sister that gives me shit all the time instead of worrying you're going to hurt my feelings. You're right too. I need to focus on getting better."

"You're right. Okay, so get your shit together, Gray. If you don't hear from Chrissy tomorrow, I'll see what the holdup is, and I'll let you know."

"Okay, love you, sis."

"Love you, too."

I walk through my house and back downstairs. Instead of doing my band workout, I jump on the treadmill. I have some frustrations I need to take out, and I might as well do that with a brisk run. I won't think about those big blue eyes, the coconut smell, or how my body reacted when Cat touched me. Nope, I'm going to completely forget about the woman that has consumed my every thought since yesterday.

## 6

# CATHERINE

"You okay?" I ask my son for the third time.

We're just leaving the baseball field, and the game didn't go well. Cole missed a ball at first base, and he struck out two of the three times at bat. And even though the whole team didn't play their best, I know my son, and he's going to be so hard on himself about the error and his performance.

He's leaning with his head on his hand against the door of the car. "Yeah, Mom, I'm fine. I just sucked tonight… I need to do better."

"Cole, language, and you didn't do badly. Everyone is allowed to make mistakes." I want to chime in that his coach is too hard on him. You shouldn't get benched just because you make one error, but that's the way his coach does it.

He won't even look at me, and it's killing me the way he's looking out the window. "I know, Mom, but his son made three errors on first base, and he didn't take him out for it. It's just not fair."

As his mom, there are so many things I want to say, but I know talking smack about his coach is not going to help in the long run. As much as I hate it, I know what I need to do. "I know it doesn't seem fair, but he's the coach, and you have to play by his rules. Everyone makes mistakes, and that's okay. All you can do is work your hardest and do your best."

He gets mad, but at least he finally looks at me. "I do work hard."

I put my turn signal on. We're only five minutes from home, but this car ride is feeling like an eternity. "Cole, playing games online all weekend long is not working hard." I hold a hand up because I know what he's about to say. "I know you deserve down time, but you spent the majority of your time in your room playing that game. Did you run? Do arm care? Stretch? Do anything to help improve your game?"

When I'm met with silence, I look over at him as I pull up to the stop sign. "I'm not trying to get on you, Cole, but you want to be better, and I'm just trying to help."

"You're right, Mom."

My mouth drops open, but I slam it shut. "Okay."

"I'll work harder," he says, and my hands tighten on the steering wheel. Did I just get through to him?

We get a few more blocks, and I bring up the one thing I know I need to talk to him about. Everything is in place. I've moved all my patients around, got the okay from the hospital to work out of the office the next two months. Everything is in place, but I still need to talk to Cole about it. "So, there's something I need to talk to you about."

"What is it?"

"You know Holden Gray?"

It's like I can see him rolling his eyes as he says, "Yes, Mom, I know who Holden Gray is."

I clear my throat. "Right, well, he's injured—"

Cole cuts me off. "Yeah, he has a rotator cuff strain, and the news is saying that he's going to be out for a while."

I should have known that Cole would already know all about Holden's injuries. "Yeah, well, I've been asked to be in charge of his treatment."

Cole shifts in his seat so fast I almost get

whiplash. "You're going to be helping Holden Gray?"

"Yeah, well, we're still working out the details, but it's going to be intense therapy. He's wanting to make it back for the playoffs, so it's a lot."

I pull into our driveway and park the car. Cole doesn't make a move for the door; he's staring at me, waiting for me to continue. "So I have two months to get his arm better, and it's going to require me to be a live-in therapist." I hold my hand up. "Now if you're uncomfortable with this at all, you can tell me, and I can get someone else—"

"Wait. Mom, are you saying you're going to be staying at Holden Gray's house?"

He looks so excited it's like he can barely contain himself. "Actually, we would be staying at Holden Gray's house."

He sits back, stunned. "Mom, you have to take it."

He's out the door and running up the front steps of our house by the time I get my door open. "Cole, where are you going?"

"I need to pack, I need to call my friends, I need to—"

I have the key to the house so he's rocking back and forth on his feet as he rambles on.

Slowly, I follow behind him. "There are a few things we need to go over, Cole. You can't tell your friends anything about Holden's therapy. I could lose my job if that happens. Second, I still need to talk to Jeremy about this—he's coming over for dinner."

For the first time since I mentioned it to him, he looks skeptical. "Mom, please, even if Jeremy says no, we both know you're still going to do it."

I put my hand on his shoulder. My son knows me well. "Well, it's for me to decide. So let's keep this between us for now, you got me?"

"I got you."

As soon as we're inside, he races off, and I holler behind him. "Where are you going?"

"To pack," he screams from the other side of the house.

Well, at least one of us is excited. I'm feeling a lot of things. Challenged, nervous, overwhelmed, and a little up in my feels about this.

I drop my purse and head straight for the kitchen. After preheating the oven, I pop in the lasagna I premade this morning to heat up.

When the doorbell rings, I make my way to the door and open it. I'm not sure what I expect. A hello kiss? A compliment? Maybe him saying he missed me? But Jeremy just nods at me. "Catherine."

I move to the side to let him in as I say his name. "Jeremy."

I close the door and walk into the kitchen. "I have lasagna in the oven. I'm going to throw together a salad. Do you want to keep me company while I get dinner ready?"

He nods and takes a seat at the table. He sits stiffly, his back ramrod straight while he pushes his glasses up the bridge of this nose.

I grab all the contents to make a salad and set them on the counter. "So how was work today?"

He goes on about spreadsheets and the state of the financial market, and I try to pay attention as he talks. Normally, I'm intrigued by what he says because who doesn't love a good spreadsheet? But today, I'm a little preoccupied.

I wait for him to ask me about work, and when he does, I figure it's as good of an opening as I'm going to get. "I actually had an opportunity presented to me, but I thought I should talk to you before I took it."

He doesn't ask any questions, just waits patiently for me to continue. I go over to the table and sit next to him. "A professional baseball player was injured and needs therapy. It's an in-house position, and I would be working with him for the next two months."

I'm holding my breath, waiting for him to respond. I'm not sure what I expect. Is he going to be mad? Is he going to tell me I shouldn't do it? Or maybe ask me not to?

He blinks at me. "And will you be compensated for your overtime?"

I sit back, a little deflated. "Yeah, I'll be paid for overtime, and there is a bonus that I'll be receiving also."

He nods once, with no emotion on his face. "You should do it."

"Oh," I say as I get up and go back to cutting up vegetables. "Yeah, well, I plan to, but just thought I should mention it to you. I wasn't sure what you'd think about Cole and me staying at his house. I just didn't want you to hear it from someone else."

He nods his head and starts talking about his appointments for the rest of the week. While he talks, I can't help but feel a little defeated. I'm not sure what I was hoping for. Of course, I wouldn't want him to tell me not to do it, but it would be nice if he at least had some emotion about it. I want him to feel some passion toward me. There aren't a lot of men I know that would be okay with the woman they're dating staying with another man. I don't want someone bossy that tries to tell me what to do, but maybe a little possessive and protective. He didn't even ask Holden's name. All he was worried about was the money.

The timer goes off on the oven, and I holler for Cole. "It's time to eat."

Jeremy doesn't miss a beat, though, and continues telling us stories about the happenings at his accounting office. Cole is practically vibrating in his seat, and I know it's from excitement. I didn't even mention how Holden said he'd work with him on baseball while we were there. I didn't want to get his hopes up in case Holden changes his mind. Holden… why can't I get him out of my head? He is definitely not the type of man that would be okay with his girlfriend staying at another man's house.

Instantly, I feel guilty. Jeremy is a good man, and I need to remember that. As we sit here and eat, I try to pay better attention to him. "So what about the fundraising dinner next week? Is it black tie?

He talks about the event, and I know I need to forget about the wild card that is Holden Gray. He may be attractive, but so is Jeremy. And Jeremy is safe, dependable… predictable.

And that's what I need.

Holden Gray will be on my caseload for two months, and then we'll go our separate ways. I'm determined to make the next two months professional. I will do my job, and then I'll get back to my real life. No brown-eyed, handsome baseball player is going to change that either.

## 7

## HOLDEN

This time when the doorbell rings, I know it's her. I don't know how I know it, but I hold my breath in anticipation until I finally lay eyes on her again. "Hey, Cat."

She scrunches her nose at me. "Hello, Holden. Can I come in?"

I move back to let her in, and instantly the smell of her coconut shampoo hits me in the nose. "Is that shampoo? I mean, the coconut?" I sound like a creepy stalker when I say it, and I can't deny that I've thought about buying the scent so I can smell it whenever. But deep down, I know it won't be the same.

"It's my body lotion."

I hold back a groan as I picture her running her hands across her body to apply said lotion. As I follow behind her, I take in her round ass in her black leggings. She has on a long-sleeve tight shirt, and her hair is up in a ponytail again. Because I can't wait a second longer, I demand, "Tell me yes."

She smirks but covers it up quickly. I point at the living room, and she goes in there and sits down in the same chair she sat down in the last time. "I've worked it out so that I could be here for the next two months, but I thought we should talk first and lay down some ground rules."

My interest is piqued. I should have known she'd come back at me with rules. She sits up a little taller. "Okay, so first of all, I will be completely dedicated to your rehabilitation while I'm here, but I will not miss any of Cole's games while doing it. They are all at night through the week and some are Saturday during the day, but that shouldn't conflict with our working schedule."

I lean forward and don't say anything, surprised by how adamant she is about this. She must take my silence as disapproval because she insists, "I haven't missed one game, Holden, and I won't start now."

I'm taken aback. Surely, that's not true. "You haven't missed one game?"

She seems offended almost. "Of course not."

"But…"

"Not one, and I won't start now. If that's a problem—"

I cut her off. "It's not a problem at all, I guess I'm just surprised. You're a good mom."

It's her turn to be stunned silent, and I realize what I said. "Shit, I didn't mean it like that. I'm not surprised you're a good mom. I'm sure you are… the best. I don't know my mom, but my foster mom never attended any of my games. It's just nice… that's all." I hold my hands up. "Anything we do here won't interfere with Cole's games. I promise you that."

When she came in, she was all business, and now she seems to relax a little. "Thank you… and I'm sorry that your mom or your foster mom didn't come to watch you play. It was their loss, Holden."

I shut my eyes tight, and it brings up a bunch of old memories. I remember always looking into the stands, hoping to find someone there supporting me during the games. When I got into the foster home with King, Dom, Gabe, Ledger, and Chrissy, they became the family I needed. They would come to games, but they were kids too. Regardless, we always made a point to be there for each other through everything.

My voice thick with emotion, I clear my throat. "What about Cole's father? Is he in the picture?" Before she can tell me it's none of my business, I continue, "Is he going to have a problem with him being here?"

She juts her chin at me. "Cole's father walked away when Cole was six months old and hasn't looked back."

"His loss," I tell her with complete honesty. How could any man be with Cat and then walk away from her?

"Right. Well, uh, what else?" While she thinks about it, I butt in again.

"What about the boyfriend?"

She's on defense again. Her shoulders stiffen, and she watches me, unsure about my question. "What about him?"

I wave my hand between the two of us. "About this? What's he think about this? Is he okay with you staying here?"

"He knows this is for work. He's fine with it."

I've never been one to hold back. I'm used to pissing people off, but it's not like I want to piss her off. I just think she should know. "He's a dumbass."

Her hands clench together in her lap, and before she can defend him, I continue. "He's a dumbass, and you deserve better. If you were mine, there's no way I'd be okay with you spending two months in a house with another man."

Of course she's going to stick up for him. "Jeremy is very analytical. He looks at things differently than most men."

"If you were mine—"

But before I can get the rest of my statement out, she interrupts me. "But I'm not yours, Holden. I'm not yours now, and I won't be in the future. I've seen the plethora of women you've been seen with—which brings me to my next rule."

I move to the edge of my seat like I'm ready for whatever she's about to say, but all I'm doing is trying to get closer to her. There's no way I'm going to be with her for two months and not make her mine. It's not happening.

She lifts her head, and her cheeks turn a rosy pink. "I know you have needs—"

I smirk at her. "You want to talk about my needs?"

She gets flustered. "No, of course not. I'm just saying that I have a thirteen-year-old boy. An impressionable thirteen-year-old boy, and I'm trying to teach him how to treat a woman."

As innocently as I can muster, I tell her in a seductive voice, "Trust me, I know how to treat a woman."

Her cheeks get redder, and it's amazing to watch as the flush carries down her neck and chest. "This isn't going to work—"

She shoots to her feet, and I do the same. I put my hand around her wrist, and when I do, we both stare at the spot where I'm touching her. I release her, holding my hands up away from her. "Sorry, I shouldn't have touched you. Uh, I get it. I'll be respectful."

She has so much doubt in her eyes when she looks at me. She crosses her arms over her chest. "Really? I won't have to worry about my son seeing you traipse women in and out of here?"

I'm completely sincere when I answer her. "Absolutely not. I'm one hundred percent focused on getting better. No women."

She's still holding her arms around herself. "And your girlfriend is okay with that?"

Surprised doesn't even cover it. I've searched online to find anything I can on her, but I never thought she would have done the same. "You looked me up?"

She rolls her eyes, and then as if she realizes it's not professional, she gives me a pointed look. "Of course I looked you up. I'm going to bring my kid around you."

"Okay." I shrug.

But that's not good enough. "So your girlfriend… is she going to be here?"

"If you mean the woman that I have dated on and off the last couple of months, no, she won't be here. She came yesterday, and I told her I wouldn't be able to play for two months. She let me know she was going to give me space so I can get better."

Her face contorts before she even realizes it. She throws a hand up. "Did she not think she should stick around to help you or be there for you?"

This is getting too deep. I never talk about myself, but with Cat, it's so easy just to tell her everything I'm thinking and feeling. Well, not everything because I think if she knew what I was thinking about her, it would freak her out. "Kendall and I were just dating, and I knew exactly why she was dating me."

If her face was pink before, it's a bright cherry

red now. She starts to stutter and stammer, and it's then I realize what she thought I meant. I could play with her a little and see if I can make her blush any more, but I can tell it's important to her that she keep this professional. "She was dating me so she could be my plus one for events. It's fine. I knew exactly what our relationship was. I'm fine that it's over."

## 8

## CATHERINE

I'm angry for him even though he acts unbothered by it all. What kind of person ends a relationship like she did? I grit my teeth and remind myself that I have to remain professional and I shouldn't get involved.

"Anyway, I was thinking that before we finalize everything, it would be a good idea for you to meet Cole."

His eyes light up. "Yeah, that's a good idea. I'd love to meet him. Let's do that."

Why does the fact that he looks genuinely happy to meet my son make my belly do a little flip? "Great, so let me go and get him. He's outside in the car."

I walk out of the house and down the front

steps, and Cole is leaning against the car. He's so excited about this, and even though I've talked to him about how we're here for a job and he's going to have to leave Mr. Gray alone, I know that Cole will be on his best behavior. "You ready?"

His eyes are wide, and he nods his head up and down. It's like he can't believe this is happening, and now the time has come for him to meet one of his idols. He spent all morning telling me what a neat job I have.

As soon as we get to the front door, I'm debating if I should knock again or not, but I don't have to make a decision because the door swings open.

Cole is practically vibrating next to me when Holden holds his hand out to him. "Hey, Cole, I'm Holden Gray."

Cole shakes his hand excitedly. "Hello, Mr. Gray."

Holden stands back to let us in. "Cole, call me Holden."

He leads us back into the living room and points at the couch. My son bounces onto the cushions, and I wince as I look between Holden and Cole. I swear teenage boys never just sit, it's more of a bounce, thud, or dive than anything else. I look around at the sturdy furniture and think surely Cole couldn't do too much damage in the two months we'll be here.

"Can I get you guys something to drink?"

"We're fine," I tell him. "Thank you."

"Sure." He looks at my son. "Your mom tells me you're a pitcher and you play first base."

"I do. I'm on the middle school team."

They talk baseball for a few minutes, and I let out a sigh of relief. I'm not sure what I expected, but I'm happy to see that they're getting along. Cole is absolutely awestruck as he answers all of Holden's questions.

"Have you guys had dinner yet?"

Shoot, I didn't even think before I came here that it was close to dinnertime. Cole and I are used to eating later because it's usually after his baseball practice. "No we haven't. We'll get out of your hair."

Holden laughs and shakes his head. "No, I was hoping you'd stay. I can order dinner, and while we wait, I can show you and Cole around the house and where you'll be staying."

Cole jumps to his feet. "I can't believe I get to stay here. Mom said you have a weight room."

Holden looks as excited as Cole. "I do. I didn't

get to show your mom the other day, but in the backyard, I have a bullpen set up, the infield of a baseball field, and a batting cage."

Cole's mouth drops, and for the first time ever, he's stunned into silence. When he pulls himself together, he's incredulous. "You have a bullpen, batting cage, and an infield… in your backyard?"

Holden laughs and points in that direction. "Do you want to see it?"

"Do I?" Cole asks as he bounces up and down. I'm so used to him trying to act cool all the time that I love seeing him like this. Happiness is radiating off him as he follows Holden through the house and out the back door.

I'm amazed at everything he has outside. We walk to a huge outdoor kitchen, fireplace, large screen TV, and couches and tables. But Cole doesn't even notice it because he's running around the backyard looking at all the things Holden has set up for baseball. Holden stands next to me with a huge smile on his face as my son races through his yard.

"I think he likes it."

I'm caught up in the moment, and my mouth betrays me. "Yeah, I think I'm going to have a hard time getting him out of here in two months."

As soon as the words leave my mouth, I know I

said the wrong thing. Is he worried we're going to try and stay or something? Irrational thoughts go through my head, and I can't avoid his gaze any longer. He has his head tilted to the side, watching me closely. I feel like I need to explain. "I mean, of course, we're leaving in two months. I just meant, he's going to love being here… while we're here… I mean, while I'm here to do therapy on your shoulder."

I wish I knew what he's thinking. He's just watching me, no smile on his face, no frown, just looking at me. He's quiet for so long that I ask him, "What is it? Why are you looking at me like that?"

He opens his mouth and then closes it, shaking his head.

I smile, but I'm nervous. "What is it?"

"I don't think you want to hear why I'm looking at you like I am."

I haven't even started yet, and I've already made it awkward. "Look, I didn't mean to make it awkward. I don't want you to think I have any ulterior motives here. In two months, we're out of here. Cole will be fine. I'll be fine. I was just commenting on how much he'll love being here… while he's here." I put my hand to my face and groan. "Oh my God, I'm making it worse. I just need to shut up."

He grabs my wrist and pulls my hands from my face. "I'm looking at you because you're beautiful, Cat."

For just a tiny sliver of a moment, I want to soak in his words, but just as fast, I know I shouldn't. What am I even thinking? I'm his physical therapist… and I'm seeing someone. I can't get all crazy because Holden Gray thinks I'm pretty. As much as I hate to, I pull away from his gentle hold. "Thank you."

I force my gaze from his and instead watch Cole as he inspects everything in the back yard. Holden is still staring at me, but I don't have the guts to look his way.

He sighs. "I'm going to order dinner. Pizza okay?"

I clear my throat. "That's perfect."

"What do you like on it?"

Cole approaches us, "Mom likes all the vegetables. Yuck. We always get a cheese pizza."

Holden walks away to call in the pizza. When he comes back, he takes us on a tour of the house. If I thought Cole was going to be spoiled with the backyard, he's definitely going to be with his bedroom. The guest room Holden gave Cole is decorated with all the awards and accolades that Holden has received in his career. There's a huge king-size bed, walk-in closet and private bathroom.

My room is next to Cole's, and it's decorated with beautiful peach walls, dark mahogany furniture, and a balcony. The bed is also a king-size bed, and I'm not sure what I'm going to do with all that room. It's huge compared to the full-size bed I'm used to.

"And here's your private bath. The shower is a rainfall shower system and has dual shower heads."

I'm nodding as I follow behind him and try not to show any reaction when he mentions this dual shower heads. We've lost Cole at this point because he's still looking at all the trophies in his room. I escape the bathroom because even though it's huge, it's still confining being in there with Holden. "Your home is beautiful."

"Thanks. I had it professionally decorated. If it was up to me it would be TVs, mini fridges, and bean bag chairs."

"Well, Cole would love that, and there's something to say about the simplicity of a bean bag chair. It's lightweight, and you can just drop it anywhere and have a place to sit." I barely resist rolling my eyes. Am I really having a conversation with him about bean bag chairs? "Thank you again for inviting us to eat dinner. Do you want to go over the schedule I've come up with while we're waiting?"

Before he can answer, I'm leading us out of the bedroom and down the stairs. I don't stop until we're back in the living room. I'm glad I saved my notes on my phone, so I open it and start discussing the schedule. We talk about running, therapy, and recovery. "And of course before we start each day, I'll stretch you out."

For the first time, Holden looks almost like he's in pain. "You're going to stretch me out?"

"Yeah, I think it's important, especially when we first start. A lot of people think they stretch enough, but most don't. This way you'll know what's expected of you."

He opens his mouth, but before he can say whatever it is he's going to say, the doorbell rings. "I'll be right back."

Shoot, I left my wallet in the car. "Here, let me run out and get my purse."

He holds his hand up to stop me. "You don't pay… when you're with me, you don't pay, Cat."

I laugh like it's a joke but then stop when I realize he's being for real. "But—"

I don't get the rest out. The doorbell rings again, but he's not going to be rushed. He leans down until we're eye to eye. "When you're with me, I pay."

I could argue with him and tell him that it doesn't make sense, but it's obvious that's not going to matter. For some reason, this is important to him. I gulp as he stares me down, and when I finally nod, he smiles at me and then goes to answer the door.

I'm trying to catch my breath when Cole comes running, and I meet him at the bottom of the steps. "Come on, we'll go to the kitchen to get plates."

As I'm grabbing plates and utensils, Holden comes in and stops at the island. Cole is already seated at a stool, and I put out the plates. We work together like we've done this before, and it's a little disturbing to my need to keep this all professional.

Holden opens a bag and pulls out a big bowl of salad, setting it in the middle. He then opens the cheese pizza box and sets it down in front of Cole. The second box he sets in front of me. My mouth drops when I see the vegetable-covered pizza. "You got me a pizza? I could have eaten the cheese."

He shrugs like it's not a big deal. "You should have what you want."

My mouth is hanging open as I stare at him. Is he for real? I think this is the nicest thing anyone has done for me in a while. Why am I getting all teary-eyed over a pizza? "Thank you," I stutter out.

He seems taken aback by my sincerity. He pulls out two pieces of pizza and puts them on my plate. "You're welcome."

We eat in silence for a few minutes, and I'm beginning to wonder if this is a good idea or not. How am I going to stay professional if he's going to do nice things for me? And even though Jeremy and I are not that serious and nothing has happened between Holden and me, I still feel guilty. I have a feeling the next two months are going to be a challenge for me and not because of my job. That I can do. It's these feelings that Holden evokes in me. These feelings I don't know what to do with.

## 9

## HOLDEN

I'm not sure what I was thinking. Did I really think I could work closely with Cat and not want more? It's been a week since she and Cole moved in, and Cat and I have spent most days together.

She wasn't joking when she said she was going to stretch me out before every exercise. Every morning, she massages my arms and legs before taking me through a routine of stretches, and then we run three miles. It's been a week of pure torture.

And this morning is not any different. "I can do this on my own."

She seems taken aback by my short attitude, and I instantly want to apologize, but the other part of me hopes she concedes. She's dressed in leggings and a tank top. Her hair is in a ponytail, and she doesn't have a hint of makeup on, but she's still the most beautiful woman I've ever seen. There's no way around it: When she works with me, she's just too close, and I'm doing my best to keep my distance from her, but it's getting damn near impossible.

"You know the rules, Holden. Until I think you're stretching enough on your own, I'm doing it for you. We don't want another injury."

Instead of getting up on the table, I rest my hands on it and hang my head between my shoulders. Not another day. "I can't do this, Catherine."

She stops next to me, but I don't look at her. "Well, this sounds serious. Catherine, huh?"

I blink and try to ready myself to look her in the eye. I finally look at her, and I can already feel myself weakening. I can't let her put her hands on me.

"I'm sorry, Cat. I just mean, I'm an adult. I can stretch myself out."

"But—" she starts, and I hold my hand up to stop her. "You don't understand."

Her hands fidget together in front of her. "Well, explain it to me. We already talked about this, so what's the issue?"

Looking into her big blue eyes, I want to lean in and kiss her. It's as simple as that. At every turn, I'm fighting this attraction, and I'm about to lose my shit. I can't let her touch me one more time. Not without me being able to touch her in return.

"You can't touch me… Cat."

It's not until I say it out loud that I realize how it sounds. Her forehead creases in worry. "Holden, I'm sorry. If I've made you uncomfortable, I promise you that was not my intention. I didn't mean…"

Her face is red from embarrassment, and she turns away from me. "I'm sorry… I didn't think I was—"

"It's not you… it's me," I tell her honestly, but she's shaking her head in disbelief.

"No, don't do that. I made you uncomfortable, and I'm glad you said something… Can you tell me what I did exactly and I guarantee it won't happen again."

I blow out a breath in frustration. How do I even begin to explain this to her? If I try, it's going to make things even more uncomfortable between us, plus I have to keep reminding myself that she has a boyfriend. I climb up on the table and lie down, my face buried into the pillow where at least

I can try to hide my moans when the time comes. "Look, just forget I said anything," I mutter.

She doesn't move, though. When I look up at her, she has her arms crossed over her chest and looks at me with a forlorn look on her face. "Cat… please… let's just get this over with."

Worry is evident on her face, and I feel like a grade A asshole. She takes this job very seriously, and I know I've hurt her by insinuating that she's done something wrong. Fuck me, I can't do this. "Listen—"

She shakes her head. "Talk to me, Holden. For real. Tell me what's going on."

I clench my eyes shut and then shake my head. Fuck it. I sit up on the edge of the bed, my legs hanging off the side. "You can't touch me… because I'm barely fucking hanging on here. I've tried to be respectful, but there's only so much a man can fuckin' take. I uh, have a reaction when you touch me… do you get my drift?"

Her eyes are round as she blinks at me. It's almost as if she's trying to figure out if I'm being serious with her. She's speechless, and I feel like a fuckin' pervert right now. "Look, like I said, it's my problem. I'll deal with it, now can we move on please?"

When she seems like she's pulled herself together, she juts her chin at me. At least she's smiling now instead of looking like I kicked her puppy or something. "Okay, so listen. It's normal… I mean your reaction can be normal. I'm stimulating—"

I groan and drop my head between my shoulders. "Please don't say that word."

She clears her throat. "Okay, so I'm touching you—"

I groan again, but she doesn't stop this time. "And you're having a reaction to it. It's fine. We'll just ignore it. I mean, this is crazy, I'm your physical therapist. I have to touch you, Holden."

Just kill me now. "I don't think you understand—"

She puts her hands on my chest and pushes me backwards while hovering over me. She starts on my legs while she continues to talk. "I understand. Your body reacts… you have an erection."

I bring my arm up and cover my face. Can this get any more embarrassing? I try to tune her out, but as soon as her fingers dig into my thigh, I sit up and shove off the table. "That's it. I'm going for a run."

Without waiting for a response, I walk past her,

ignoring my half-hard cock, and make my way through the house, out the front door and start running down the road. She thinks this is a normal reaction, but it's not. This is not just random response; it's because I like her.

Not until I get a few blocks do I realize that Cat is trailing behind me.

"You're going to pull something, Holden Gray. This is too fast of a pace."

It's only when I hear her huffing and out of breath that I slow down. She matches my pace, and we do the rest of the run without talking. I don't even look at her out of my peripheral vision. "You need to run with more clothes on, Cat."

She slows down for a second and then catches up with me. "If you have a problem with the way my body jiggles when I move, then don't look."

I give her a heated look, and it's then she gets it. Hell, I need her to cover her body. It's not that I have a problem with her body; it's that I like her body a little too much.

She lifts her eyebrows, and her mouth forms a perfect circle. "Oh."

I nod and focus on the road in front of me. "Yeah, oh."

The rest of the run is in silence, and when we

get back to my house, we get into our routine. She does needling on my shoulder, and I just close my eyes and let her do it.

When we're almost done, she fills the silence. "I'm going to be out tonight. But don't worry, I'm taking Cole to my house."

I want to ask her where she's going, but it's not my right to ask. I'm sure she's going out with her boyfriend, and just the thought makes me crazy. As far as I know, she hasn't seen him since she moved in here. Instead of asking her what I want to know, I ask about Cole. "Why are you taking Cole to your house?"

"Well, I don't expect you to watch him while I'm out."

My jaw tightens because I hate to even think about her being out with another man. "He's thirteen. He's a good kid, and he doesn't need a sitter."

She puts her hand over her heart. "Aww, thank you, Holden. He is a good kid, right?"

I nod. I've only been around her and Cole for a week, but she's a great mother. She talks to him, not at him, she helps him with his homework, she is all in with his baseball practices and games, and it's obvious she loves him. "Yeah, he's a good kid because you're a good mom."

I swear she gets misty-eyed, and I continue. "Let him hang here with me. I'll invite my family over, and we'll cook out and do a game in the backyard."

She bites her lip worriedly. "You know you can't throw yet, right? We'll start a throwing plan next month."

I nod. "I got it. No throwing." When she's still hesitant, I rub my hand through my hair. "If you don't want to leave Cole with me, I—"

She holds her hand up to stop me. "Of course I trust you, Holden. I wouldn't be here, living in your house, if I didn't."

After she removes the needles from my skin, I sit up. "All right, well, I'm going out for a few hours. I'll be back when Cole gets out of school."

"You don't have to watch him—"

I cut her off with a look. "I'll be here, Cat. Have fun with whatever you have going on tonight."

Before she can respond, I walk away. It's either that or I'm going to kiss her until she's breathless and she realizes that Jeremy is not the right man for her. I am.

## 10

## CATHERINE

I haven't seen Jeremy in a week. I spent the time getting Cole and me into Holden's house and then on top of the one time a day therapy sessions, the runs, the strength training, and Cole's practices, well, there wasn't much time to see Jeremy.

But tonight is a planned dinner with his accounting firm.

As the doorbell rings, I finish putting on my lipstick and make my way downstairs. Both Cole and Holden are standing inside the door, and I rush down the stairs to meet them. I'm about to do introductions when Holden holds his hand out. "You must be Jeremy. I'm Holden."

Jeremy pushes his glasses up his nose and then

reaches for Holden's hand. "Yeah, it's nice to meet you."

Jeremy looks at Cole. "Hello, Cole."

Cole just raises his hand in a half wave and mutters, "Hey, Jeremy."

I push my arm through Jeremy's. "Well, we better go. Cole, please be good tonight. Call if you need anything."

"You look beautiful, Cat," Holden says, and I practically stumble on my feet.

"Thank you. I'll be back later. Let me know if you, I mean Cole needs anything."

I'm quiet as we walk to the car, and I realize that Jeremy didn't comment on how I look. It's not that I need a man to notice me to know my worth, but it does feel good to get complimented.

The whole thing is awkward, and as I look back at Cole and Holden and see Holden has his arm around Cole's shoulder, I wish that I was staying home with them instead of going to what will probably be a boring dinner.

As Jeremy drives us across town, he is telling me about who I'm going to meet and how I should act while I'm there. He goes on and on, and I can't help but think about everything. Jeremy doesn't open the car door for me. He doesn't open doors for me at all. He doesn't hug me or kiss me unless we're in complete privacy. We've only been seeing each other a little while, but I don't expect things to change. I feel guilty as I look over at him. He's completely clueless to where my thoughts have gone. *I bet Holden wouldn't keep his hands to himself.*

I let out a small gasp and turn to look out the window. I'm not sure where that thought came from, but now that it's in my head, I can't get it out.

"Catherine," Jeremy says, and I realize I totally zoned out.

"Sorry, Jeremy. It's been a long week. What were you saying?"

He smiles wide and nods his head. "I get it. I'm sure dealing with the jock is exhausting."

Instantly, I come to Holden's defense. "No, that's not what I meant. Holden is nice and a hard worker. I just meant it's exhausting with the change in my schedule, Cole's schedule, and everything else."

Jeremy doesn't respond; he just purses his lips and continues driving. The rest of the ride is in silence, and I'm actually thankful when we walk into the dinner party to deal with some of the awkwardness.

Jeremy stops and talks to a few people, and I

wait for him to introduce me. After the third person stops and my date has continued to ignore me, I get irritated. When another man comes to talk to Jeremy, I stick my hand out. "Hello, I'm Catherine Maples."

The man is congenial, but I can hear Jeremy huff next to me. I give him a look that says *What's your problem?* before continuing the conversation.

When we finally make it to our seats for dinner, Jeremy excuses himself almost immediately.

I'm shocked as I sit here, looking around the room where I don't know anyone. I mean, it's Whiskey Run, so chances are I've seen most of these people before, but I've not talked to them. I straighten my back and look around the room. Jeremy is gone so long, mingling with other people that I'm about to get up and walk out when the speaker announces for everyone to sit down and that dinner is being served.

Jeremy sits next to me, and I lean toward him. "What's going on?"

He's confused by my question, but before I can explain it to him, the other people at our table sit down.

Conversation continues, and Jeremy turns to the woman sitting on the other side of him.

Shocked by the way he's ignoring me, I stare down, debating what I should do, until the man next to me nudges me with his arm. "Hello. I'm Clark."

He's holding his hand out, and I shake it. "I'm Catherine."

"I don't recognize you from any of the locations, and I would remember you."

I point to Jeremy. "I'm here with Jeremy." *Even if he's not acting like it*, I think silently.

Clark looks at Jeremy and then back at me with a nod. If knowing I'm here with another man cautions him, he doesn't let on because he spends the remainder of the dinner talking to me. Any time there is a break in the conversation, I look at Jeremy, but he's paying me no mind. I'm not sure why he asked me to come if he planned to ignore me all night long.

After dinner, I'm ready to call it a night, even if that means I need to call an Uber, but the speaker walks out onto the stage while dessert is being served. Darn it, if I get up now, everyone will know I'm leaving.

I sit and listen as they announce the quarterly winners, and I clap when everyone around me claps. There's a few speeches, and just when I think the night is about to end, they announce that the dance floor has opened up.

I lean toward Jeremy. "Are you ready to go?"

He rolls his eyes. "Don't be rude, Catherine. I'll be ready to go in fifteen minutes."

He turns back to the woman next to him, and I start to fume. This is crazy.

I get up to leave, and Clark puts his hand on mine. "Dance with me."

"No, really, I was just about to leave. Thank you for talking to me during dinner, it was nice to meet you."

He doesn't take no for an answer and pulls me onto the dance floor. He's been a perfect gentleman all evening, and he did save me from having no one to talk to during dinner. "Fine. Once dance and then I really must go."

He spins me on the dance floor, and by the end of the song, I'm laughing and smiling. Clark is a wonderful dancer, and it's the most fun I've had all night.

As he twirls me back into his arms, he leans into me, pressing his hard manhood into my hip. "Come home with me."

I put both hands on his chest and push. "No, I'm here on a date."

His voice is calm, but he's strong, and he doesn't let me go. "Your date has ignored you all night long. Come home with me… I know how to treat a woman. I'll have you screaming my name before the night is over."

I stomp my heel into the top of his foot, and when he bellows in pain, the people around all stare at us. I push away from him and try to keep my shit together. I hate to make a scene because it will be all over town by morning. "Oh, I'm sorry. I'm a horrible dancer. Now I must go."

I stomp over to the table. "Jeremy, I'm leaving."

I grab my purse, and fuming, I walk toward the front door. I don't stop when I get outside, I just keep walking. Hell, I'll walk home if I have to. I'm almost out of the parking lot when Jeremy comes running up behind me. "Catherine, where are you going? Hold on and I'll get the car."

I throw a hand out. "I'll find my own way home, Jeremy."

"Shoot," he mutters, and I assume he's left me be, but it isn't long before he's pulling his car up next to me.

"Get in."

I keep walking. "I'll get myself home, thank you very much."

"Catherine, don't be ridiculous. It's ten miles, and it's dark outside. Just get in and I'll take you home."

I look down at the stupid heels I'm wearing and I know my feet won't make it ten miles. I huff and then walk in front of the car, open the door, and get in. "I want you to take me straight home."

He pulls back out on the road and is driving slowly. "What happened back there? Why are you acting like this?"

I turn, staring daggers at him. "Why? Why am I acting like this?" I'm flabbergasted because he's serious. He doesn't have a clue. "Jeremy, I was your date tonight, and you completely ignored me. You didn't introduce me to anyone or include me in any conversations, and then—" I huff out a breath, trying to contain myself, but it's impossible to do. "And then your friend Clark, propositioned me."

Finally, he shows some emotion. "Propositioned you?"

"Yes, he wanted to take me home with him. I had to stomp his foot and shove him for him to let me go."

His hands tighten on the steering wheel. "Oh, Catherine. I wish you wouldn't have done that.

Clark is harmless, and he's the vice president of the company."

My mouth drops open, and I just stare at him. Is he for real right now? He has to be joking. "I'm sorry, are you telling me I should just let him hit on me?"

He pauses. "Well, no, I mean, I'm just saying…."

I hold my hand up. "Please stop talking. Just take me home, Jeremy."

The rest of the car ride is in silence. I'm steaming mad, and I can feel myself about to lose my cool. As soon as he pulls into Holden's driveway, I'm opening the door before he gets to a complete stop. I jog up the steps, ignoring Jeremy calling to me from his window. He thinks he wants to talk to me right now, but he doesn't. Right now, he'd see a whole new side of me. Nope, I'm going to calm down, and then I'm going to give Jeremy a piece of my mind.

## 11

## HOLDEN

My face hurts from smiling so hard.

I can't remember the last time I've enjoyed myself like I am tonight. Of course, I keep thinking about Catherine and the fact that she's out with that Jeremy, but after meeting him, I can't bring myself to feel threatened. He didn't even notice how beautiful Cat looked tonight.

My brother King bunts the ball and takes off running around the bases. He slides into second, and when Cole gets him out, he gets up and limps back to us.

"King, please don't hurt yourself," Haven exclaims.

He groans. "I'm too old for this."

Haven just laughs, rubbing her slightly rounded

belly. "I hope not. I'm pretty sure your son will want you to play with him."

And just like that, King stops limping and picks Haven up with a spin. They kiss, and I have to force myself to look away. It almost feels like I'm invading on a private moment.

Dom and Gabe are trying to coach Cole on his pitching technique, and I elbow my sister. "You having fun?"

She crosses her arms over her chest. "I am. I love being here with you guys. It's like we're a real family."

I put my arm around her shoulder. "We are a real family, Chrissy."

She nods, but her smile doesn't quite reach her eyes. "Right." She gestures toward Cole. "He's a good kid."

I can't help but agree. I haven't been around a lot of teenage kids, but I already know Cole is special. To see the way he is with his mom and just how he carries himself tells me that he's a great kid. "He's the best."

Of course, my sister the matchmaker can't stop now. "His mom is pretty great too."

"Tell me about her boyfriend."

Chrissy huffs her breath, and I realize she's

probably not going to spill the beans, but I can't resist asking. "You should ask her."

How do I explain to her that I'm doing my best to keep my distance from Cat? I want to know what she sees in Jeremy, but I don't want to know really. Hell, I don't even want to think about her with another man. "I could ask her, but I figure it's safer asking you."

She doesn't get it. "Safer? What's that supposed to mean?"

I groan, not completely happy with myself. "It means I like her. I like Cat, and if I talk to her about her fuckin' boyfriend, then I'm going to go off."

Chrissy gets that look in her eye. "You like her? Of course you do. You were deadset on no one moving in here, and you didn't hesitate moving her—and her son—in immediately."

I cross my arms over my chest and stare at Chrissy. I know I've already asked her about Jeremy and she said she couldn't tell me, but I knew once I got her in person, she would give in.

She groans and throws her head back. "Holden! Fine! His name is Jeremy Tabor, he's an accountant, and I've only met him a few times, but he's super dry. No sense of humor at all."

I frown. "Is he good to her?"

She shrugs, scrunching her nose up. "He's… fine, I guess. He's not mean to her, but look, honestly, they seem more like friends than anything else."

At that, I hear the screen door open, and when I turn, Cat is walking out of the house. She's still in her dress and high heels, and I'm not sure how to explain it, but she looks frazzled. Immediately, I walk over to her. "You okay? How was your date?" I try to leave the displeasure out of my voice, but I can hear it.

She takes a deep breath and lets it out slowly. "It was… fine. What's going on out here?"

With my hand on her lower back, I lead her off the porch, and my family all comes to stand with us. "Cat, I want you to meet my family. You know Chrissy. And these are my brothers Gabriel, Dom, and King and my new sister, Haven."

"My wife," King adds.

We all laugh because the man is all kinds of obsessed over his wife. "Right, your wife."

Cat is looking between all of them. "Wow, there's so many of you. Okay, Chrissy, Gabriel, Dom, King, and Haven. Right?"

I nod. "There's one more, actually. Ledger is enlisted right now."

She repeats his name. "Ledger… got it."

"Mom, go get your glove and come play."

My mouth falls open. "Your glove? You play?"

Before she can answer, Cole chimes in, "Mom plays with me all the time. She's pretty good."

I look at the woman in awe as she holds up her finger. "Okay, I'm going to change and be right back."

She jogs away, and as everyone goes back to the game, Gabriel nudges my shoulder. "Close your mouth, you're drooling."

I snap my mouth closed, and Gabe has his arms over his chest, watching Cat walk away. "Have you told her how you feel?"

I roll my eyes. "No, I haven't told her I want to fuck her."

He laughs. "I think there's more to it than that."

"I don't do long-term."

He widens his stance, nodding his head. "Right. Well, if that's the case, stay away from her. She has a kid. She doesn't do flings."

I know he's right, but there's no way I can stay away from her. It's like she's in my blood. I have to have her. Maybe, just maybe I can be up front with her and tell her what I want and get her out of my system. I turn to my brother. "What about you? What's going on in your love life?"

Automatically his eyes shift across the yard toward Chrissy. "I don't have one."

I look between him and my sister. "What—"

But before I can even finish my question, his phone starts ringing, and I remember that it's his emergency ringtone.

Gabe looks at his phone. "There's a fire. I gotta go." He looks out at our family, and they've all stopped what they're doing and are now looking anxiously at him. We all worry when he gets a fire call. "See you guys later. Keep working, Cole! You're a natural, and if you keep it up, you'll be following this guy into the big leagues."

He gives a longing look at Chrissy and then is headed out the door. All of us are quiet, and I'm sure we're each saying our own prayers for his safety.

They are just getting back into the game when Cat walks out in cut-off shorts and a tank top, holding a pink glove.

"Pink?" I ask her.

She smiles up at me. "It's cute, right?"

Before I can tell her she's the one that's cute, Cole hollers for her to join them.

For the first time, I'm glad I have to sit out because I can stay here and watch Cat. There's something about the way she smiles and laughs. She gives a hundred percent, and when she dives for a ball and misses, she gets right up and chases after it. My family is totally rooting for her, and she's won them all over in no time.

It's crazy because if she was anyone else, I would be trying to figure out how to get her out of here. But with Cat, I'm wondering how long I can keep her and Cole here. It doesn't make sense to me, but I will not question it. I'm just going to enjoy it while I can.

## 12

## CATHERINE

I can't sleep because I can't stop replaying the night in my head. I should probably figure out what I'm going to do about Jeremy—I can't keep seeing him —but that's not what is on the forefront of my mind. Nope, all I'm thinking about is how wonderful it was hanging out with my son, Holden, and his family.

At one point, I sat back while everyone was playing the game and just soaked it all in. This is what I hoped for my son to have. This is the kind of family nights I wish he had. Everyone was laughing, having fun, joking around with each other. The night was perfect.

I walk into the kitchen and turn on the low light, trying to be quiet. Holden and Cole are asleep, and I don't want to wake them up just because I can't sleep.

I pull open the fridge and grab a bottle of water. When I shut the door, I jump and let out a squeal after seeing Holden standing behind the once open door.

"You okay?"

With my hand to my chest, I try to calm my breathing. "Yeah, I'm fine. You scared me."

He walks across the kitchen, putting the island between us. "Sorry. I couldn't sleep."

"Me either… why couldn't you sleep?"

He puts his hand to his shoulder and grimaces. He'll never admit it out loud, so I shake my head. "You're hurting, aren't you?"

He grunts and lifts his shoulders in a shrug.

"Really? Answer me, Holden, instead of grunting and groaning."

When he remains silent, I ask, "Did you throw the ball tonight in the game with your family?"

"I did not throw the ball," he assures me.

He's hiding something, though. He was standing with Chrissy when I got here, but maybe he played before then. "What did you do, Holden?"

He lets out a laugh. "I may have hit a few balls—"

I start to cut him off, but he continues. "I was helping Cole with his batting."

I stomp my foot. "Really? What part of resting your arm do you not understand? I'm trying to get your arm ready, and you don't want a setback."

Once I get started, I can't stop. I keep rambling on, and he's just sitting on the stool with a smile on his face.

"What? What is it? Why are you looking at me like that?"

He juts his chin at me. "You're cute when you get all riled up."

I groan in frustration. "Do you need a pain pill?"

He holds his hands up and shakes his head. "Nope, no pain pills."

I haven't been able to get him to take any of his pain pills, so I know what I need to do. I tap him on the shoulder. "Fine, take your shirt off and sit down at the table. I'll be right back."

I walk downstairs to the therapy room. I grab the massage ointment and the gua sha tool so I can do some scraping therapy.

When I get back into the kitchen, he's in the same spot I left him in. "I'm fine. I don't need any—"

"Forget it. Let's go, mister. Shirt off and in the chair. I'm not going to let you set yourself back. Let me do this."

His jaw tightens, and I half expect him to refuse, but he finally gets up. As he walks toward the table, he takes his shirt off. I watch as his muscles ripple and clear my throat when he turns around to look at me.

"Sit," I insist.

He sits down, and I add ointment to my palms and then rub my hands together to warm it up. I barely touch his shoulder and he groans. I make a point to work his muscles, and when I can feel him loosen up, I use the scraper. His satisfied groans turn into painful moans, but I don't lighten up. "You'll probably bruise, Holden. I can feel the knots forming already."

He doesn't answer; he just lets me work my magic.

He's quiet as I work, and when I notice he has his eyes clenched, I ask him, "You okay?"

His brown eyes open and stare up at me with so much turmoil. "You think I should call it quits?"

I lay the scraper down and then go and grab a dish towel to clean him up. "I thought we talked about this. The plan is for you to go back and then decide whether you're going to stay or not."

He doesn't try to hide the worry in his face. "I hit a few balls and look at me. The pain is overwhelming. I can't continue like this."

After I clean the ointment off his shoulder, I sit down in the chair next to him. "I know it's frustrating, Holden. I need you to give me time. It's a strain, and it needs time to heal."

He's giving me a skeptical look, and I'm trying not to get frustrated. I understand how he feels, but mindset is half the battle. "If you don't believe you're going to get better, you won't."

"But—"

I shake my head and cut him off. "No, seriously, I need you to get rid of the negative thoughts. I need you to picture yourself playing in the playoffs. Getting outs, making plays, and hitting bombs."

With that, he smiles. "Bombs, huh?"

I shrug. "Is it called something different in the major leagues? That's what Cole and his friends call home runs."

He nods at me. "No, that's right. We call them bombs too. I just thought it was cute when you said it."

I lean back in my chair. The fact he's attractive

and that he is good to my son makes him even harder to resist. I have to keep reminding myself that this is my job, and I can't screw it up… no matter how handsome and charming the patient is.

Holden slides his hand across the table, and right before he touches my hand, he stops. I stare at the small space between our fingers and wait.

He clears his throat. "How about you? How was your date?"

His question jars me, and I pull my hand back. "Fine."

He laughs. "Fine? That's what you said earlier. I don't think it was fine. You seemed, I don't know, frazzled when you got home earlier."

When I remain silent, he asks worriedly, "Did something happen?"

I lean back in my chair and cross my arms over my chest. If I was working from the office, I could talk to my friends during lunch about this. I haven't had a chance to talk to them, and I really need to talk to someone. Without even thinking, I just blurt it out to him. Before I realize it, I have told him the whole sordid story. I told him about Jeremy ignoring me, about dancing with Clark and his proposition, and how I put my heel into his foot for him to release me.

"Who the fuck is Clark? What's his last name?"

He's so mad his whole body is tense. Every muscle in his chest is pulled tight, and I can feel the anger radiating off him. "It's fine. Trust me, you should be worried about his foot where I stomped it. I'm fine."

"He shouldn't have… fuck, Cat, what did Jeremy do?"

I never expected this reaction from Holden. I'm so surprised by the anger in his voice, I answer him without even thinking. "He didn't want me to offend Clark… he's like vice president of the company or something. I don't know."

He scoots his chair back, and the loud screech fills the room. "That mother fucker… Are you kidding me right now? He didn't kick Clark's ass? Well, fuck it, I will. Where do Jeremy and Clark work?"

I suck in a breath and just stare at him. I've known Holden Gray a little over a week, and already he's more protective of me than any man has ever been. I can feel the tears forming in my eyes, and if I blink, they're going to run down my cheeks.

He leans forward and wraps his hand around my forearm. "Cat, where can I find this Clark? And fuck, Jeremy too, because I want to both tear their faces off."

I cover his hand and squeeze it. "Holden, stop. It's not your problem. I'm fine. I took care of it myself."

He reaches his other hand up to my face, cupping my chin. "You shouldn't have to. Do you know that, Cat? You shouldn't have to take care of yourself. No man should be able to touch you if you don't want them to. Your boyfriend shouldn't let any other man touch you."

"Holden, stop. I'm okay. I'm okay," I keep telling him, but he doesn't let go of me, and he doesn't seem to calm down any. He scoots his chair toward me and he pulls me to him until our foreheads are resting against each other.

He's taking deep breaths, and I pull back. "Holden, you're too upset about this… it's not a big deal."

He grabs my hands and holds on to them. "It's a huge deal, Cat. Don't you get it? You deserve to be treated with respect, and if this Clark… this Jeremy… doesn't get that, then someone needs to explain it to them."

A tear rolls down my cheek because I can't hold it back any longer. I've never had someone make me feel the way Holden does. It feels good to have someone on my side. I tighten my hold on his hand. "I won't see Clark again, so I don't need to worry about him… plus that was handled. As for Jeremy, I'll take care of it." He starts to say something, and I stop him. "And if I need your help, I'll tell you."

He doesn't like it. He wants to argue with me about it, but he doesn't do it. "Okay, Holden. I'm fine, I promise. Please just forget this… I appreciate you… I really do, but I'm okay."

He's looking at me, searching my face, and when he focuses on my lips, I wonder if he's going to kiss me. For just a second, I'm about to lean in, and then I catch myself. I'm his physical therapist, and no matter how nice he is, he's a player. Absolutely nothing will come of this. I can't let it.

## 13

## HOLDEN

One month down, one to go.

The last four weeks went by so fast. I really wish time would slow down. In less than a month, I'll be back on the field, and Cat and Cole will be gone.

I just finished my stretching, and Cat walks into the therapy room, smiling ear to ear and clapping her hands together. "Are you ready to start throwing?"

I suck in a breath but nod my head. My arm feels good. Hell, it feels better than it's ever felt, but I'm still nervous.

Cat doesn't seem nervous at all. She's worked me hard this past month, and she feels confident in my abilities. She sticks her thumb up and points at the door. "Come with me."

But I don't follow her. "What? Right now? We're throwing now?"

She shakes her head and smiles. "No, I want to show you something first."

She doesn't wait for me. She turns on her heel with a bounce and then practically skips out of the room. I follow behind her, trying to ignore the way she looks in her leggings and tank top. I made a point to keep my distance from her, especially after everything with Clark. I don't want her to be worried that I'm going to expect anything from her even though I want her more every day.

As I follow her into the living room, she turns on the television. "I've been watching tape."

I look between her and the TV. "You've been watching tape?"

She laughs and then sits down on the sofa. "Yeah, sit down and let me show you."

I sit down next to her, and she pulls out her phone. She screen shares a video to the television. "This is you four years ago. Watch your arm."

She shows a short video and then shows another. "This one is from three years ago."

She then shows another. "Last year."

I tune into the television, but I'm not seeing

whatever it is she wants me to see. "What are you showing me?"

She gets up and moves to the television, sitting down in front of it. "Okay, watch and I'll slow it down." She points at my arm slot as she replays the video.

"Three years ago. Look at your arm. See how it doesn't go back as far as the year before?"

She plays the two videos again, and I can barely notice it. "Okay, look close, here you are four years ago." She plays it and then plays another video. "This is from this season. Look at your arm slot. You've been slowly losing flexibility in your arm. There's a lot of reasons for this, but mostly it's from overuse and lack of stretching. I'm going to record you throwing today, and I'm pretty sure you're going to see a difference."

I have her play the videos over again, and I see exactly what she's talking about. How did I miss this? How did my trainers miss this?

We go outside, she sets up her camera, and after warming up, she wants me to throw to her from twenty feet away. "I can't throw with you, Cat. I'll hurt you."

She rolls her eyes and shoves her fist into her pink glove. "It's not like you're pitching to me.

We're tossing the ball, just checking your arm out and seeing how it feels."

We toss the ball back and forth, and as we throw, she slowly starts putting more distance between us. "How does it feel?"

I nod and throw it again. "Good. I feel good."

"Good, now try and throw it a little harder."

"I don't—"

She puts her hand on her hip. "You're not going to hurt me. Throw it, Holden."

I pick up the speed, and we toss for a few more minutes. "Good, now let's watch."

Instead of going back inside, she grabs her phone and plays back the video. As she points at my arm, she cheers. "Yes, look at that, Holden. Look at your arm. The flexibility is there. How's it feel?"

I roll my shoulder, and there's absolutely no pain. "I feel good. Fuck, it feels really good."

She jumps up and down. "All right, that's it for throwing today."

I point out at where we were standing. "But I could go—"

She laughs and takes my glove from me. "It's a throwing plan, Holden. Can we do it my way? Don't worry, we're going to increase it, but this is good for today. Now let's go and do some recovery."

I want to push myself, but Cat has proven she knows what she's doing. I've given her my all this past month, and I'm going to continue to do so. "Sure, let's do it."

I follow her back to the therapy room and mentally prepare myself for the torture that is coming. Her hands on me is torture, but it's become an addiction.

## 14

## CATHERINE

Sitting in the stands, waiting on Cole's game to start, I'm surprised to see Holden talking to the coach by the dugout.

I wrap my arms around my knees and try to focus on the kids warming up on the field, but I can't help but watch Holden. He stands out among all the men surrounding him.

There are other moms sitting close to me on the bleachers, and they're whispering about "the new guy with the coach." I don't think any of them realize he's Holden Gray, the catcher for the Jasper Bears.

I hear the words "hot," "sexy," "whose dad is that?" and "I'd like to take him home with me."

Instantly, I feel anger and bitter jealousy rise

inside me. It's not like I have the right to be jealous. There's nothing going on between Holden and me, and I have no claims to him whatsoever. Probably if he did know that I had even a hint of jealousy, he would fire me on the spot. So I sit here quietly and just let myself simmer.

I watch as Holden walks away from the coach. Two of the moms stop him at the bottom of the bleachers, and I barely resist rolling my eyes. I mean, can they be any more obvious? Their giggling and flirting carries across the stands for everyone to hear.

"Are you a new coach?" I hear Anita ask. "My son is Timmy, he plays short stop."

"Nope, not a coach," he says, giving away nothing.

Of course, Kylie is not having that. She's the biggest gossip of all the moms, and she'll sleuth out all the information she can so she can pass it around. "Are you the dad of one of the boys on the team?"

Holden shakes his head. "Nope, not a dad. I'm friends with Cole and Cat."

All heads turn to me, and when I finally brave a look at Holden, he's staring straight at me. I didn't even realize he saw me here, but it's clear he did.

He found me immediately without even searching. The way he's smiling has me melting in my seat. Why does he have to be so dang handsome?

He steps away from the two women and walks up to where I'm sitting. He sits right next to me, his leg against mine. "Hey, Cat."

Goosebumps. I have freakin' goosebumps on my arm, and it's eighty-five degrees outside. "Hey, Holden."

He nudges his shoulder against mine. "How you doing?"

I clear my throat and am about to answer him when he leans down to whisper into my ear, "You have goosebumps. You cold? Or is it something else?"

I hold my tongue because everyone around us is eager to find out what is going on. The way Holden's looking at me, he knows exactly why I have goosebumps. I whisper harshly at him, "What are you even doing here?"

He measures me with a look and then stares out at the field where the game is starting. "I came to watch Cole play. If you want me to sit somewhere else, I can."

I put my hand on his leg and then jerk it back really quickly. I don't need to add any fuel to the fire. "No, stay, I'm sorry. I'm sure Cole thinks it's the coolest thing ever that you're here."

I wrap my arms around my knees and look at my son standing next to the dugout. He's waving up at us, and I'm shocked, but I wave back. With a grimace, I mutter to Holden, "He usually ignores me. I guess the wave was thanks to your presence, but I'll take it any way I can get it."

His voice is low. "Trust me, if there's a kid that loves his momma, it's Cole. You two have a good relationship."

I don't know why it matters, but his opinion goes straight to my heart.

Holden looks around the field. "Where's Jeremy?"

I don't take my eyes off the field. "He's not coming. He doesn't like baseball." I inhale deeply. "Plus, I broke up with him."

His head whips around so fast. "You did?"

I nod, and he's smiling ear to ear. "So you're a free woman?"

Oh God, I'm not even sure what to make of that comment or the way he's looking at me. Does he think since I broke up with Jeremy that I'm going to fall into his bed now? I mean, of course I want to, what woman wouldn't? But he's a player…

and I'm his physical therapist. "I'm still your therapist," I remind him.

He grunts. "For another month."

I look into his big brown eyes and repeat what he said. "For another month." I already know that leaving his house and not seeing him every day is going to be hard, and I don't want to think about leaving him or our time being over.

He opens his mouth, but something catches his eye. He smiles and then apologizes to me.

"What are you sorry for?"

I should be curious what he's looking at, but I've found that when Holden is around I stayed glued to him. It's not until I feel the bleachers shaking that I look, and I can't contain my surprise. King, Haven, Chrissy, Gabe, and Dom are all coming up the steps, and they greet me and Holden before sitting down surrounding us.

"Where's Cole?" King asks as he searches the field.

I'm about to answer in the dugout when Holden replies, "He's pitching the first two innings."

My mouth falls open. "How do you know that?" We're up to bat right now, but the coach is notorious for not letting anyone know when they're pitching.

Holden clears his throat and looks at me with a guilty expression. "Cole mentioned that the coach never told him when he was pitching and would usually throw him in without letting him warm up. I got here early today to work with Cole, and I talked with the coach about it."

"What did you talk about, exactly?"

He scrunches up his nose. "Well, I explained to him the importance of stretching and warming up and the impact it has on keeping the arm healthy. I just asked him that when he has Cole pitch that he gives him a heads-up."

I stutter and point to myself. "I had that exact conversation with him last season, and nothing changed."

Holden nods his head. "That's what Cole said. Look, I don't want you to be mad. I wasn't trying to overstep…"

I put my hand on his forearm. "Mad? I'm not mad. I appreciate what you did, Holden. I mean, yeah, it sucks that the coach blew me off, but what's important is my son's arm. So yeah, thank you. I really appreciate you doing that."

I'm looking at him, and automatically I'm even more attracted to him. This is crazy, and I know it is, but no one has done something like this for me and Cole before.

Haven taps me on the shoulder. "Look, there he goes."

I watch as Cole jogs to the mound. I've seen it plenty of times, but I can see a difference in him this time. He has a swagger to him, and he's holding his head high with confidence, and I know exactly who to thank for that.

I watch Cole on the mound in awe. He strikes out the first batter. The second batter hits a ground ball to the shortstop and gets thrown out at first. The third hitter hits a ball over the second baseman's head, and the runner makes it to first. I gasp and watch Cole, waiting for him to react. I know he worries if someone gets a hit and it puts more stress on him, but he seems to shake it off. The fourth batter gets up to the plate, and I'm holding my breath. He swings at the first pitch and the ball comes right back to him. He catches it and jogs off the field.

Holden puts a hand to my back. "Breathe, baby. You gotta breathe."

I shake my head. "That was—"

I stop talking when Cole looks up at us into the stands before he goes into the dugout. He gives us a short head nod, and Holden gives him a thumbs-up in return. "What? How?" I start, but I don't even know what I'm asking.

Holden shrugs, but the pride on his face is clearly there. "I worked with him on his pitching." He holds his hands up. "And no, I didn't throw with him; I just helped him with his mechanics, that's all. But it's him that put the work in."

Our next three batters strike out, and in no time, Cole is back on the mound. He throws a nine pitch inning allowing no runs. He's so proud of himself I can practically see him vibrating with it. As he comes off the mound, Holden pumps his fist in the air. "Way to throw it, Cole."

Cole's smile gets even bigger, and I want to throw my arms around the man sitting next to me. I know I can't do that, though, so instead, I put my hand over my heart. "Thank you, Holden. You don't know what this means to me… I mean, just… thank you… really."

He reaches over and squeezes my knee. "You're welcome, honey."

I have to force my eyes back to the game because if I keep sitting here, looking into his big brown eyes, I'm going to kiss him, and I know that would be a mistake.

15

## HOLDEN

We won. I mean, Cole's team won, but why does it feel like I won? I'm standing next to Cat, surrounded by my family, and we're all on our feet, cheering when we win the game.

You would think it's the world series by the way the boys all dogpile in the middle of the field.

Gabe, King, and Dom are all giving me high-fives, and Haven and Chrissy are hugging Cat. As soon as they release her, I grab Cat and haul her against me. I'm not surprised in the least that she fits perfectly in my arms. This feels good and right on so many levels.

I hate to release her, but if I don't, I'm going to embarrass her and kiss her right here in front of everyone. "I'll be right back."

I walk off the stands and go to the side of the dugout. "Hey, Coach. Congratulations on the win. I'm going to order some pizzas from the Pizza Haven. Wanna bring your team to celebrate?"

Before he can answer me, the players that overheard me ask start cheering, and the coach laughs. "Yeah, sounds good. Thanks, Holden."

I don't want to embarrass Cole with his friends, so I go back out of the dugout and pull out my phone. I dial the number for Pizza Haven and give them a heads-up we're coming and order thirty pizzas. That should be enough for the players and their families. At least to get started. I reach Cat and my family at the same time Cole does. My brothers and I all high-five him, and he hugs his mom, Haven, and Chrissy. The kid is smiling ear to ear and is talking a mile a minute. All I can do is smile with him and soak it all in.

"We're going to Pizza Haven," he announces to Cat.

Her eyes widen. "We are?"

Cole nods. "Yeah, Holden invited the whole team."

Shit, did I just fuck up? "Is that okay? I should have asked you first, right? I got caught up in the moment and the celebrating."

"Holden, the whole team? Do you have any idea how much that's going to cost?"

Fuck she's something else. She has to know that I have money, but she's worried about me spending it. "I got it, no worries, Cat. We're celebrating."

King slaps me on the shoulder. "Little brother's buying? We're in."

Gabe chimes in, "Hell yeah."

Chrissy shrugs. "I'm in."

Dom is the only one that declines. "I have a motor to put in early in the morning, but good job tonight, Cole. Way to throw it."

Dom and Cole slap hands, and everyone starts to make their way to the parking lot.

I convince Cat and Cole to ride with me to the restaurant, and by the time we get there, the restaurant is putting pizzas out on tables. Some of the players are already here, and Cole runs off to join them. We're greeted by the manager, and I hand over my credit card. When she says the total, Cat gasps beside me. "No, Holden. Here, I can pay for it."

She's reaching for her purse, and I put my hand on hers to stop her. "Don't you dare, Cat."

She's shaking her head with determination on

her face. "No way, it's not happening, Holden Gray. This is too much."

She fans her hand around as the servers bring out more pizzas, and I wrap my hand around hers, pulling it to me. "What did I say? You're with me, you don't pay."

"Holden, that's ridiculous. I can't let you pay for all these people."

I lean down, and I'm so close that all I can think about is kissing her. Being next to her all evening is making me crazy. "I think we've talked about this. When you're with me—"

She cuts me off, rolling her eyes. "I don't pay when I'm with you. I hear what you're saying, but it's not right. I can't let you."

I have to touch her. I put my hand on her cheek, and do I imagine it or does she lean into my palm? "Let me do this, Cat. I want to do it."

She blinks her blue eyes at me. All I have to do is lean down a few more inches and I could have my lips on hers. Yeah, she's my therapist, but she's no longer with Jeremy. There's nothing stopping me now.

"Mom!" Cole hollers, and it brings me out of my trance. I release my hold on her and excuse myself while she and Cole talk.

I walk over to the counter. "Can I get game cards too? Just leave the tab open. I'll close it before I leave."

The manager thanks me, and after some back and forth, I find Cole and hand him the cards. "Here, buddy. Make sure your friends and their siblings get one. Let me know if you need more."

He looks at me as if I've just hung the moon. "Thanks, Holden."

I want to hug him. I've never been a guy that's overly affectionate, but there's something about this kid and his mom that brings it out of me. "You're welcome, bud."

Not wanting to embarrass him, I hold my hand up and fist-bump him. He takes off, and by the time I find Cat again, she's sitting at a big round table with my family. Instantly, she scoots over so I can sit down next to her. It's a tight fit, but I'm not complaining because I like being this close to her.

My family is all ribbing each other, and they've already started on their second pizza, but Cat has a plate saved for me. "Thank you."

She laughs. "I think I'm supposed to be thanking you."

"Sir, here's your veggie pizza."

I thank the server and set the small pizza down

in front of Cat. She looks between me and the pizza. "You got me—"

Fuck, when she looks at me like that, I can barely control myself. "You should have what you want, Cat."

I put a slice of her pizza on a plate and slide it in front of her, and the whole time I'm wishing that I was something she wanted.

We stay for hours. Parents come over to thank me for dinner, and I see the way they look at Cat and me. That's good. I've seen the way some of these guys look at Cat. I want them all to know she's taken… that she's mine.

## 16

## CATHERINE

As I walk into the living room at Holden's house, I'm still on a high. Seeing my son happy tonight means everything to me. I should go to bed. Heck, I should have been in bed hours ago, but I'm just too ramped up from the night.

"Well, he's in bed, but I don't see him going to sleep for a while." I stop next to the sofa that Holden's sitting on. "Tonight was a good night."

Holden is still smiling. "It was a good night."

"Thank you—"

He sits up and holds his hand out. "Nope. No more thank yous. I wanted to treat Cole and his friends. That was a hard win. They deserved it."

I sit down on the couch, and even though there's a half of a cushion between us, my heart still feels like it's galloping in my chest. This man is something else. "No, I mean, yeah, thanks for dinner and feeding all Cole's friends, but I'm talking about what you did for Cole. I'm not sure what you did, but you made a difference in him."

Holden scoots to the edge of the couch, excited. "Yeah, he pitched lights out. I was super—"

I raise my hand up to stop him. "Yeah, he pitched well, but that's not what I'm talking about. I can see a difference in him since he's been here. There's a confidence in him and well, he's a good kid. He's always been a good kid, but he's standing up for himself now, and well, thank you."

Holden tries to blow it off. "I didn't do—"

I laugh, because I can't help it. "Don't say you didn't do anything. You working with him means everything. I know you should be focusing on your health and your game, but you took time out for my kid. I just, I want you to know I appreciate it… more than you'll ever know."

He's listening to me now, and he nods his head. "I know you do, but I'll be honest with you, Cat. He's a good kid. That's all you. All I did was help him with his game."

I wish he could see the difference he's making. It's not just his game he's helped him with. It's always been hard for Cole that he doesn't have a male figure in his life. I try to do it all and play both roles, but it's not the same. "It's more than that. And I mean, your whole family, the way they all showed up tonight for Cole."

I stop because I know if I continue, I'm going to cry.

Holden is nodding his head, smiling. "Yeah, my family is pretty awesome."

"Tell me about them. I know Gabe is your biological brother. Tell me how the rest of you all met."

"We were all in the same foster home. King, Ledger, Dom, Gabe, and I had been in multiple homes through the years. I was eleven and Gabe was ten when we got placed in the same home as King, Ledger, and Dom. They sort of just took us in. We worked the system and we knew that we wouldn't be separated after that. We took care of each other."

"And Chrissy?"

"Uh, we were there a few years before Chrissy came to live with us. She was eight, I think. She ended up in a house full of boys, which is pretty wild when you think about it. Anything could have happened to her."

He's thinking about it, and the fear is plain on his face. I reach over and put my hand in his. "But nothing happened to her, Holden."

He squeezes my hand. "Yeah, we all took care of her. We protected her. She was almost adopted twice but messed it up both times. She didn't want to leave us."

"Wow," I exclaim with surprise.

Holden's nodding, like he's lost in memory. "Yeah, at the time, we wondered if she'd be better off in a home with a mom and a dad, but she was not having it. She ran away, and Gabe is the one that found her. She wouldn't come back until he promised her that he wouldn't let anyone take her from us." He laughs. "It was a lot of work and a bunch of shenanigans, but we kept our promise to her."

I should let go of his hand, but I don't. "Yeah, I think it worked out. Chrissy's an amazing woman."

He nods, but I see the regret on his face.

I tap his hand and then release it. "Hey! Where'd you go? What are you thinking about?"

He shakes his head and then looks at me. I try to hide the fact I'm attracted to him, but I can't help but wonder if he knows. He slides toward me. He's not touching me, but he might as well be. He's so close I can feel the heat radiating off of him. "I need to talk to you about something."

I pull back, surprised. I'm not sure what he's about to say, but I mentally try to prepare myself for it. Is he going to tell me he's having pain? Is he going to say he's found someone else to do his therapy?

I take a deep breath. "Sure. What is it?"

His voice is husky, and he's looking at my lips. "I like you."

I wish I could say I have a normal reaction, but I don't. My heart does a little flip. My palms get sweaty, and I feel like I can't catch my breath. I need to be cool about this because even though I feel the same way too, I know nothing can happen between us. "Uh, well, I like you too, Holden, but…"

He leans toward me. "No but. We like each other."

"But—"

He cuts me off again and laughs. "Cat, tell me the truth. Do you feel the attraction between us?"

The way he's looking at me with heated curiosity, I can't lie to him. "Yeah, I'm attracted to you, Holden. But I don't date patients."

"I'm your patient for one more month."

I hate thinking of this ending, but I know it has to. He's right; there's only one month left of this, and then Cole and I are moving back home. Would it be so horrible to have fun while it lasts? As soon as the thought comes, I push it aside. "Holden, I have a son to think about, and I wouldn't want him to get the wrong idea."

He reaches for my hand and holds it between us. His thumb is wreaking havoc on my skin. "Wrong idea about what?"

For the first time in forever, I want something I can't—I shouldn't—want. I'm a rule follower and always have been. Me wanting Holden is not a good thing, and there's no way I can give in to my desires. "This would be a fling. This is a temporary situation and then you'll go back to your career and forget about me." He starts to talk, but I hold my hand up. "No, don't give me any promises that you can't keep. I know what this would be, Holden, and no matter how much I want to give in, enjoy it while it lasts, I can't let myself."

He brings one hand up and cups my cheek. If he wasn't touching me, this would be so much easier. His thumb brushes back and forth lightly across my cheek. "Really? You're going to end this before it even gets started, Cat?"

When his thumb lightly strokes across my lip, I gasp because it's so intimate. We're looking into each other's eyes, and it's like I can feel his touch everywhere. My body comes alive when he looks at me like he is. I barely get the words out, and they sound hesitant and unsure. "This is a bad idea."

It's as if he doesn't hear me because he leans in. "I'm going to kiss you now."

He doesn't hesitate. He leans in, and as soon as his lips touch mine, I know it's no use resisting him. His lips are firm against mine, and his hand tightens at the side of my neck. His tongue slides across the seam of my lips, wanting entrance, and I let him in. The kiss goes from a simple peck to an intense ravaging of my mouth. His tongue slides along mine, and I groan as he lifts me like I weigh nothing and pulls me to his lap. I'm straddling him, and I'm flush to his body, my breasts pressed into his chest and my core lodged against his hips. A shifting of my hips has me gasping as his manhood presses against me. I gasp and pull away from him, trying to get off his lap, but he doesn't let me. We're both heaving, wide-eyed, staring into each other's eyes. Shock is evident on his face, and it's exactly how I feel.

"Holden, you have to let me up."

He tries to calm his breath and nods his head. "I will, I'm going to let you up, but first I need to know you're not going to walk away from me."

"I won't," I promise him.

He sets me on the couch next to him and holds my hand, threading our fingers together. I try to pull myself together, but this is all too much. I've never wanted to do something I shouldn't more than I do right now.

"This can't happen."

He barks out a laugh. "Really? Because after that, I really think this needs to happen. That kiss was everything, Cat."

I blink up at him. I know how the kiss made me feel, and he's right, it was everything, but there's no way it affected him the same way. I don't believe it. "I agree… it was good but…"

He practically spits the words out. "Good? Fuck, Cat. It was perfect. My heart is still beating so hard it's about to come out of my chest. Feel."

He puts my hand over his heart, and sure enough, I can feel the erratic beats under my palm. I've never wanted anything as much as I want this, but there's too much at stake. "Holden…"

He knows that I'm about to tell him no, and he shakes his head. "Don't answer me yet. Just think about it. Promise me that you'll at least think about it."

I nod and pull my hand from his. I stand up and put some distance between us because if I don't, I'm not going to have the strength to keep resisting him. "I should go to bed."

He nods. "Me too."

I almost make it out of the room when he stops me. "Dream of me, sweet Cat."

Looking at him across the room, I can still see the desire in his eyes, and I know I have the same look in mine. "Good night, Holden."

And then I escape… before I do something foolish and ask him to take me to his bed.

## 17

## HOLDEN

I woke up this morning with a new determination about me. Yeah, I'm going to kick my injury's ass, but it's more than that. I have a whole new purpose. I'm going to put the work in and make it back to the playoffs. I need to prove to myself that I can do this and prove that I'm worthy of Cat and Cole. It was one kiss, but it's all I needed to know that Cat is the one for me.

When I walk into the therapy room, Cat is already in here. She is adjusting and cleaning equipment and won't look at me. I can't help but wonder if she thought about us at all last night, but I don't want to pounce on her first thing. I sit down on the chair and wait for her to come to me. Our eyes meet in the mirror in front of me, and I smile at her. Hell, how can I not? She's fuckin' beautiful, especially when she's blushing like she is right now. "Did you sleep okay?"

She nods. "Yeah, I slept good. Cole was still ramped up this morning when I took him to school." She taps me on the shoulder. "Take off your shirt."

I pull my shirt off and toss it to the chair in the corner. I try to ready myself for her touch. She warms the ointment in her hands and massages my shoulder.

I look at her in the mirror, taking her all in. She's in leggings and a tank top. Her blond hair is piled on top of her head. Her cheeks flush when she touches me, and I give her a few minutes of silence before I ask her the question I've wanted to ask her all night.

"Have you thought about us?"

She's staring hard at my shoulder, avoiding my gaze in the mirror. "You were serious about that?"

"Yes, of course I was serious about it. I've thought about that kiss all night long, Cat. We're good together, you can't deny it."

She blows out a breath. "It's a huge conflict of interest."

I'm grasping at straws because there's no way

I'm going to take no for an answer. "When we're working, we're working. This, between us, will be separate."

She finally looks at me, and it's then that I see the tiredness in her eyes. Maybe she didn't sleep as well as she said she did. I know it took me forever to go to sleep because I couldn't get the feel of her out of my head. "There's more to it than that, Holden."

"Like what?"

She's silent for so long that I'm sure I'm going to have to convince her. She surprises me when she lays her hands on my shoulders and seeks me out in the mirror. "If you want to do this, we need to be upfront and honest about the whole thing."

I'm nodding, wanting to get up and take her in my arms, but I stay seated. "Of course."

"I know what this is—" she continues, and I hold my hand up to stop her.

"What does that mean? You know what this is?"

She pecks me on the shoulder. "We spend time together and well, you know, but no one can know. And when we're working, we're working. Only when the therapy is done do we... ya know."

I turn in my seat and look up at her. I feel like this is too important of a conversation to be talking to each other in the mirror. "I'm not going to secretly date you, Cat. And what do you mean, you know what this is? What do you think this is?"

She doesn't even hesitate, and she's so confident with her response. "I know exactly what this is, Holden Gray, and I'm not going to let you act like it's anything more. It's a fling. We'll have some fun, and then when you go back to your career, this is over." She holds up her hand when I start to talk. "That's all I can offer you. I have my son to think about, and I won't get his hopes up just to tear him down. So that's it. If you're okay with those terms, then we can do this as long as it doesn't interfere with your therapy. If you have a problem with it, then we act like that kiss last night never happened."

I stand up and tower over her, pressing my chest to hers. She doesn't back down and leans her head back to look at me. Fuck, I have to kiss her, and I will but in due time. "You think we could just forget last night—forget that kiss ever happened?"

Before she can answer me, I wrap my hand around her neck. "Because I know I can't. Kissing you is all I've thought about, Cat. I went to sleep with my cock hard last night thinking about how perfect your lips… your body felt against mine. You want to keep this between the two of us for now, that's fine, but eventually, once I'm back and the job is done, I'm going to tell any and everyone that you're mine."

Her mouth drops, and she starts to talk, but I seal my lips to hers. I swallow her gasp, and thankfully, she doesn't resist me. She seems as lost in the kiss as I am. I want to take her right here right now, but I don't want to rush her.

Her curvy body rubbing against mine is enough to put me over the edge, but I pull back so I can look at her. "Fuck, I'm trying to abide by the rules here, honey, but I'm going to have trouble keeping my hands off you."

She's breathless. "We need to run, Holden. We need to do your workout."

Her mouth is saying one thing, but her body is telling me something else. Her nipples are hard, pressed against her shirt. Her eyes are a dark blue and filled with desire. She wants me, and I would do anything to be able to take her upstairs to bed with me, but I'm not going to spook her. I release my hold on her and take a step back. My cock is hard, tenting my shorts, and I'm not shy as I grab it and adjust myself. "You're right. Give me five minutes and I'll be ready. We'll get our workout in, eat lunch and do whatever other torture you have planned for me, and then you're mine, Cat."

She's walking backwards, putting more distance between us. I get it, though, because being this close to her is a temptation I can barely control. "And we keep this between us," she reminds me.

I shrug. "Between us," I agree, even though I silently add, *for now*.

## 18

# CATHERINE

Already, this is affecting my job.

I'm not sure if it's the sexual chemistry, the anticipation, or the way Holden is looking at me like he's going to bend me over and take me, but I'm completely off kilter from all of it. I keep telling myself to keep it together and focus on the job, but that's a little harder now knowing that in just a few hours, I can be making out with the sexiest man I've ever laid eyes on.

"All right, again."

Holden has his hands on his head, sucking in deep breaths. "You're fuckin' killing me today, Cat."

Damn it. Am I being harder on him now? Shit, see, I can't do this. All this cooped-up physical energy is making me crazy. I'm overthinking things, questioning the whole workout now, and Holden puts his hands on his hips. "You're thinking too hard, Cat. You're not being too hard on me."

"How did you—"

He comes over and puts his finger on my forehead and draws a line down it. "Because you're all scrunched up here, and you do that when you're worried about something."

I cross my arms over my traitorous chest. Just being near Holden and him innocently touching me has my body reacting. "Get back to work, Gray."

He holds his hands up and chuckles. "Got it. I'll listen to what you tell me to do, honey, but just know in the bedroom, I like to be the one in charge."

I suck in a breath, and it's like I've been hit right in the stomach. The images that come to mind are too much, and I have to shake my head to clear it. "Come on, I'll run it with you."

I take off running, and he falls in step beside me. The rest of the workout is uneventful, and I'm thankful that he keeps it professional. I'm weak when it comes to Holden, and I could easily see myself giving in to him without a lot of pressure.

We get back to the house, eat, shower separately,

and then we meet back in the therapy room and do more bands for recovery.

"How's it feel?"

He rolls his shoulder to test it out. "It feels perfect."

I take a deep breath. "Okay, let me massage it and then we'll be done for the day."

I wanted to make sure we don't cut therapy time short and it looks like we're going to actually go over a little bit. I put the ointment on my hands and then start on his shoulder. The way he groans has my stomach pulled tight, and I can't help but wonder what he sounds like in bed.

I have to force my mind elsewhere or else he's going to know exactly what I'm thinking. I work the muscles in his arm, and we're both silent while I work. When I can't stand the quiet a second more, I ask him, "What do you have planned for the rest of the day?"

Shit. That is the wrong question to ask when I'm trying to get my mind off of things. Instead of answering me, he asks his own question. "Are we done here, Cat?"

I grab a towel and wipe off his arm. "Yeah, we're done."

I'm turning away from him when he wraps his hand around my arm. "Stay."

I take a deep breath and turn around to look at him. I want this, but I didn't expect it to happen quite like this.

"Lie down."

I look at the therapy bed he's getting up from and I point at it. "You want to do it here?"

He pulls me against him, and his hand goes to my waist. I'm not a small woman, but the way he touches me makes me feel almost dainty and protected. "Fuck, Cat. All I've thought about is getting inside you, but I'm not going to bend you over a table and fuck you—"

He stops talking, and his eyebrows raise as he takes in my reaction. My heart is racing and my breath is coming in little pants. Just the thought of him bending me over the table has me wet with arousal. He leans down and kisses my forehead as I try to suck a breath into my lungs. "You like that, don't you? You want me to fuck you on this table, Cat?"

All I can do is blink up at him. My nipples are hard, and with every breath I take, I feel them graze against his chest. His voice is husky, and his hot breath hits my ear as he whispers, "My plan is to fuck you in every room of this house, Cat. But right now, I want to make you feel good. Get up there."

He pats the therapy bed, and I look between it and him.

He laughs, puts his hands at my waist, and lifts me up on the bed. "Lie down on your stomach."

I open my mouth to argue with him, and he shakes his head. "Lie down, Cat. Let me take care of you for once."

I reluctantly move to lie down on my stomach. "But I don't need—"

He puts his palm on the small of my back and pushes me until I'm lying flat on the bed. "You're always taking care of me, let me make you feel good."

As soon as his hands smooth across my back, I realize this is a bad idea. The satisfied groan leaves my mouth before I can stop it, and I bite my lip to hold back anything else that may come out. He pats me on the back. "Take your shirt off."

I flip my head around to look at him. "What?"

The look in his eyes is a challenge if I've ever seen one. "Take your shirt—and your bra—off."

"Holden, I don't think—"

He cuts me off. "That's exactly right. I don't

want you to think. Do it, Cat. Take your shirt off. I dare you."

Now I'm usually level-headed and don't succumb to dares and games, but right now, I don't want to resist him. I don't want to be level-headed and responsible. I roll to my back and pull my shirt up over my head and drop it to the floor. My eyes meet Holden's, and his brown eyes are practically black as he stares back at me.

I give him a smirk and roll back to my stomach, unclasp my bra, take it off, and drop it on top of my shirt, the whole time concealing my breasts from him. He groans and swats me on the ass. "Fine, but it's not like I won't be seeing them later."

Instantly, my lower belly pulls and anticipation builds as I think about what may happen later.

He warms the massage lotion in his hands, and as soon as he touches me, my whole body is tense. He rubs up and down my back in long, firm strokes. "That feels amazing," I moan.

We're both quiet as he glides his hands across me. I'm doing my best to just lie here when what I want to do is roll over and pull him on top of me. I groan and clench my eyes closed, trying to get myself under control.

"You okay?"

I'm tight-lipped and mutter, "Yeah, it's just hard lying here with your hands on me."

He grunts. "Now you know how I feel."

I open my eyes and stare at the floor. "What do you mean?"

His hands pause for a minute and then pick up again. "Do you have any idea how hard it has been for me to have your hands on me knowing I can't do anything about it? You drive me crazy, Cat."

"I didn't know… I just thought…"

I let my voice trail off because I don't want to admit to him that I thought I was the only one affected by it. I thought when he talked about it the one time, it was just a natural reaction to stimuli… not that it was because he wanted me. I've done my best to keep things professional even though I've been going crazy on the inside. But this whole time, I thought it was one-sided.

His hands feel so good on me, and when I'm pretty sure my body is going to burst into flames, he gruffly says, "Roll over, Cat."

I lift my head with a jerk. "But…"

"I want to see you."

I suck in a breath and roll over to my back. My plan is to avoid his gaze, but when he groans, my eyes fly to his. "Damn, Cat. You're fucking breathtaking."

His hand comes up, and he grazes the back of his hand along the side of my full breast. My nipples pucker, and I hold my breath and bite my lip to hold back my whimper.

Holden's breath quickens. "I need to touch you."

I give one simple nod, and he palms my breast, kneading my full flesh in his hands. It's like a shock to my system, and my back arches off the table, pressing myself fully into his hands.

He groans, hovering over me. "Kiss me," he demands.

I jut my chin at him with a challenge. "You kiss me."

He wastes no time in pressing his lips to mine. He groans against my lips. "Let me in, Cat."

As soon as my lips part, he takes full advantage. His tongue slides along mine, and I moan at the contact. It's like I can feel him everywhere as he ravages my mouth and rolls my nipple between his fingers. My hands come up, and I wrap them around his neck, holding him to me. Now that he's started, I don't want him to stop. When he pulls away, he doesn't go far. He kisses along my neck and collarbone, and when he suckles my nipple into his mouth, I throw my head back in ecstasy. "Yes."

He palms one breast while suckling the other, and I rub my legs together to create the friction that I need. "Holden… please," I beg of him.

"What do you need, baby? Tell me what you want."

"You. I want you," I tell him as I lift my hips up, needing to feel his touch at my core. His hands slide down my waist and across my belly, and he palms my pussy. My hips jerk, and I lift up, pressing into his touch.

He lifts his head to look into my eyes. "You're wet, aren't you, baby?"

I nod my head, and he brings the heel of his hand against my swollen clit. I grab on to his forearm because even through my clothes it feels so good. "Please…"

I start to plead with him, but the shrill of the doorbell chiming through the house slams me back to reality. I practically jump off the bed, grab my shirt, and pull it to my chest. "Oh my God," I exclaim as I stare at Holden. *What am I doing? What am I thinking? I can't do this… it's wrong on so many levels.*

"I gotta go." I turn on my heel, ready to escape to my room. I get up the stairs and to my bedroom door when I realize that Holden is right behind me. I turn to look at him, putting my hand on his chest. He's put his shirt back on, but it doesn't matter. His body is permanently etched into my mind by now.

"Cat, wait."

I pull my hand back because even touching him is too much for my senses right now. "I can't… we can't…." I stutter.

He puts his hands to my hips. "I'll get rid of whoever it is and we can—"

I shake my head side to side. "No…" The doorbell rings again, and I try to push him out of my room. "Go get the door, Holden."

He's not in any hurry. "If they want to see me, they'll wait. We're not done here."

His phone rings, and he pulls it from the pocket of his shorts. "What?" he grunts.

There's a pause. "Yeah, hang out. Give me five minutes."

He ends the call and shakes his head. "That's Jerry…" He runs his hands through his hair. "He's pissed because I've been avoiding his call."

I point toward the front of the house. "Well, go let him in. We can talk about this later."

He doesn't budge an inch. "No, I'm not moving

from this spot until I know you're not going to run from me."

I cross my arms over my chest. "This was a mistake."

He grips my waist and slams me against his body. His hard manhood prods against my belly, and my body reacts by curling into him. He pulls me in like a magnet, and even if I wanted to, I couldn't walk away from him. "Listen to me, Cat. This is not a mistake. Everything between us is so right… don't say it's a mistake."

The doorbell rings three more times in quick succession. "Holden." I give him my stern voice, the same one I use on Cole when he's not listening to something I say, but it doesn't have the same effect on Holden.

He leans in and kisses me until I'm breathless. This is not like the other kisses. It's like he has something to prove, and he doesn't stop until I have my arms wrapped around him, holding on to him for dear life. The shirt that I'm still holding to my chest has fallen, and my erect nipples are scraping against the material of his shirt. When he pulls away, he's smirking. "Fuck, everything about this is perfect, Cat. This is happening."

As I search his eyes, I know there's no way I can

resist him. I give him another shove and pant, "Go answer the door."

He's watching me closely. "Not until you tell me that this is not a mistake."

His lips are swollen, and I know mine look the same. "This is not a mistake."

His smile is instant. He kisses me again, just a quick peck. "All right, I'm going to go talk to the guys. I'll be back."

He takes a step away and then looks back at me. It's then I realize I'm still just standing here with my shirt at my feet. He looks me up and down like he could devour me. "Cover up, sweet Cat. If my friends see you like that, I'd have to gouge their eyes out."

My hand tightens on the door as he looks at me with possession in his eyes. I should hate it, but if anything, it makes me want him more, and before I can stop myself, I lift my chin at him and drop my arms to my side. "You're the only one I want looking—or touching—me, Holden."

He groans, shaking his head. "I can make them go away and we can continue this."

I step back into the room. "Nope, you go. We can do this later."

He doesn't budge, though, and I know I'm

going to have to be the one to put an end to this. His phone starts to ring again, and I smile. "Go. We'll talk about this later."

I shut the door before he can respond, and as I lean my back against the hardwood, I try to act like this is not a big deal and that I can handle a little fun with Holden without getting too attached.

## 19

## HOLDEN

My teammates are passing the beers around that they brought. There's a baseball game on the television, and everyone is talking at once. I'm smiling, nodding my head, and trying to act like I'm part of the conversation when in reality all I want is to kick them all out and go back to Cat.

Fuck, she's everything, and I'm so consumed by the idea that I'm going to fuck this up that it has me stressed out. I've never been in this position before. I'm usually a fuck em' and walk away kind of guy. Not that I mislead anyone because I always make sure the girl knows what's up. But Cat is different. I want more with her, and she's the one that is keeping her guard up.

A pillow from the couch comes careening

toward my face, and I catch it at the last second. "Gray. Earth to Gray. You listening to us?"

I toss the pillow back at Foreman, our second baseman. "Yeah, I'm listening. What's up?"

He is smiling, but the intensity in his face tells me that his question is serious. "You going to be back for the playoffs?"

A smirk is frozen on my face, not wanting to show any doubts or my insecurities. Instead of answering his question, I ask one of my own. "The question is are you guys going to get us to the playoffs?"

"Hell yeah!"

"Fuck yeah!"

"We got this in the bag!"

After the guys all chime in, they stare at me, waiting for my answer. I want to lay it all out for them and tell them everything I'm thinking about coming back and this being my retirement year, but these guys don't want to hear it. They want to hear that I'm going to help them clinch the winning spot. "Yeah, I'll be ready by then."

Yates and Carter go back to watching the game, but Foreman's eyes are glued on me. "We need you on the field, Gray."

I shrug. "I know, but Mitchell is doing a good job."

I've watched the guy standing in for me to catch in the games, and he doesn't have the same game as I do, but I've also been doing this a lot longer. He doesn't frame it like me, and at times, I've thought he's been a little lazy behind the plate, but he's getting the job done.

"He's getting by, but he's not you. When you're on the field, the whole dynamic changes. The team respects you. When you're behind the plate, you call the game, and we need that." He leans in and half-whispers, "I know you've been watching the games. We're barely holding our shit together."

He's being completely serious, and worry is etched on his face. I'm nodding my head at him, wanting him to know the truth. "You're right, Foreman, when I'm out there, I call the game but it's not because I'm behind the plate. Yeah, of course it helps, but you can do it from second base too. Be a leader. Take control and communicate with your team. Let them know what's expected of them and keep them accountable. That's all I did, and maybe you all listened to me because I've been doing this so long but yeah, I've been watching the games, and you all just need someone to stand up and take charge… That's it."

He lifts his shoulder in a half-shrug. "It's worth a shot. Something has to change."

I give him an encouraging nod. "Do it. The team needs you to step up, Foreman."

He leans back in his chair, and it's obvious his mind is going a thousand miles a minute. I know exactly what he's feeling. He has the weight of the team on him, and he takes that feeling seriously. I'm about to offer more encouragement when Cat walks in the room, and all eyes are on her.

Almost instantly, her eyes land on me, and she doesn't look anywhere else. "Hey there, sorry to interrupt, I was just letting you know I'm going to go to Cole's practice. I'll be back soon."

She's freshly showered, and besides a gloss to her lips, she's makeup free. She looks beautiful, and I'm not the only one that thinks so.

"Whoa, whoa, whoa… who is this?"

Carter stands up and with his hand held out, walks across the room toward Cat. I'm up in an instant and move to fit between them. Cat looks between me and Carter. "Uh, hi, I'm Catherine Maples, and I'm Holden's physical therapist."

I give her a look. Of course she's going to

introduce herself as my therapist. I'm not sure why I expected—or hoped—for anything else.

Carter shakes Cat's hand and holds on to it a little too long. "Catherine Maples, it's nice to meet you. I'm Josh Carter."

I move next to Cat, forcing Carter to drop his hold on her. "Cat, this is Yates and Foreman."

She gives them a little wave, and I put my hand at her waist. "Come on, I'll walk you out."

I'm rushing her out the door and don't stop until we're next to her car. She's laughing, holding her hands up. "Okay, okay, we're out. Geez, Holden, what's up with you? Did you think I'd embarrass you or something?"

She says it lightheartedly, but the way she's looking away from me instead of at me, I can see that she's bothered by the whole idea of it. I put my hand on her chin and force her to look at me and tell her point blank, "No, I'm not worried about you embarrassing me. If you stayed in there another second, with Carter's hands on you, I was going to embarrass myself. I don't like other men touching you… and just so you know, I would never have introduced you as my therapist."

Her mouth drops, and her hand goes to her chest. "Oh my goodness, Holden. I wasn't thinking. Maybe you don't want people to know…"

I let my hand slide from her chin to the side of her neck, and I hold on to her as I move closer until our bodies are touching. "What? You think I don't want people to know I'm going to physical therapy? Hell, the whole fuckin' world knows that… no, I meant that I wouldn't have introduced you as my therapist… I would have introduced you as mine."

She lets out a small gasp. "Yours?"

I nod and lean down until my lips are almost touching hers. "Yep, mine. You may be fighting it, but you're going to be mine, Cat."

She takes in a shaky breath, and I can't hold back any longer. I press my lips to hers, and it's only when I feel her arms circle around me and her fingers dig into my skin that I let myself go and show her exactly how much I want to claim her.

There's a car horn that goes off somewhere in the neighborhood, and I reluctantly pull back. "Don't go. I'll get rid of the guys and—"

She cuts me off. "I have to go… Cole's practicing and—"

"I'll tell them I have to leave and I'll go with you."

She shakes her head, smiling. "No, you need to

spend some time with your teammates. I know you're missing the game, Holden. Go in there and talk to them. I'm picking up dinner, can I bring something for everyone?"

I grumble, and it's then I know I'm losing it. Even the thought of her doing something—even as little as bringing food home—for another man makes me crazy. "Nope, they'll be gone by then. I'll grab me, you, and Cole food. I want to hear about his practice anyway."

"Holden… I can buy dinner."

I run my finger across her now swollen lip. "Not when you're with me, Cat."

She rolls her eyes. "Fine. We'll be home around seven. Now go and enjoy being with your teammates and tell them to get their game together. I can't do another nine innings of sitting on the edge of my seat. They barely squeaked out that last win."

"I'll tell them."

I kiss her again and stand in the driveway waving at her until she pulls out. I have a whole new fire under me. It's only now, after hearing her talk, that makes me want to be on that field and her cheering for me. I want that… I want to look up into the stands and see her and Cole and know they're there for me. As I make my way back inside, I'm determined to light a fire under my teammates because one way or another, they're getting to the playoffs, and I'm going to make sure I'm there to play.

## 20

CATHERINE

"Have you told him yet?"

I laugh and shake my head. I've never seen this side of Holden. He's so excited that he can barely contain himself. "No, I didn't tell him. I thought you should be the one."

He walks to the door of the kitchen and hollers up the stairs, "Cole, you about ready?"

Almost instantly I can hear Cole stomping down the stairs, and he comes into the kitchen with his backpack on and a smile on his face. This has been planned for a week, and he's excited to be going to his friends' house to spend the night. "I'm ready." He grins.

Holden is nodding his head. "Okay, so I know you're staying the night at Brad's, but I was wondering if you two would like to do something before you went to his house."

My laid-back child shrugs his shoulders. "Yeah, sure. What's up?"

Holden leans against the wall. "Well, I thought you and Brad may want to go check out the Bears game tonight."

Cole's mouth drops. "The Bears game? Tonight?" His mouth is hanging open, and he's so surprised he doesn't know what to do.

Holden smiles, nodding his head. "Yeah, I thought we could get there early and I could give you a tour of the locker room before the game. And then I thought we'd sit in a box—"

Cole's eyes get even bigger. "Like a VIP box?"

Holden nods. "Yep, I had them stock it with food, but of course you guys can order whatever."

Cole literally clutches his chest. "Are you for real right now?"

Holden nods. "Yeah. You want to call Brad and see what he thinks?"

I'd already called Brad's parents so they knew what was happening, but I let Cole walk out of the room to call his friend. As soon as he's gone, I put my hand over my heart. "Do you have any idea what you just did for my son? Thank you, Holden, really. Thank you for doing this… I hope you guys have a great time."

Holden shakes his head and walks over to a box on the top of the kitchen counter. "You act like you're not going."

I point to myself. "Oh, am I invited? I just thought…"

I let my voice trail off as he pulls some jerseys from the box. "Nope, you're going with us." He hands me a shirt. "Here you go, put this on."

I grab the shirt. "Are you sure about this? I don't want to ruin boys' night or anything."

He crosses his arms over his big barrel of a chest. "First of all, you could never ruin anything. Second of all, I want you to go. I want to sit side by side with you at the game."

I hold the shirt up. "I'll be right back."

I go up the stairs and don't realize I'm holding my breath until I'm behind my closed door. I remove the shirt I'm wearing and pull on the jersey over my tank top. I put on some jeans and tennis shoes and after reapplying my makeup and tousling my hair, I look at myself in the mirror. I turn to the side and then point my butt at the mirror, wanting to see myself from all angles, and seeing the name Gray on my back is like a jolt to my system. All of a sudden, I feel hot all over, but before I can analyze any of it, I hear Cole hollering up the stairs, "Come on, Mom. I'm going to Holden's truck."

"I'll be right there," I holler back, and then after taking a few calming breaths, I grab my purse and walk downstairs. Holden is waiting for me by the front door, and I stutter to a stop when I see him looking me up and down.

"What is it?" I ask him, pressing down the front of my shirt as I try to figure out what he's looking at.

He twirls his finger. "Turn around."

I turn my back to him, and he grunts. I look over my shoulder. "What is it? Something wrong? It's too tight, right?"

He clears his throat and walks toward me. "No, it's perfect. I like seeing my name on you."

I want to tell him that I like it too, but I just shake my head. "Oh, you're a charmer."

He pulls me into his arms. "I'm serious, Cat. I've seen hundreds of women wearing this same jersey, but it's never affected me how it is right now. It just does something to me… the rest of the world thinks you're just wearing my jersey, but me, I see you in this and it says you're mine."

It feels like my heart does a flip in my chest. I

want to challenge him and tell him that nothing can come of this… it's a fling and nothing more, but I don't say any of those things. I wish I could claim Holden, but it's just too risky. I reach for the front door. "We should go."

He seems disappointed, but he follows me. We ride the thirty minutes into Jasper with two excited boys in the back. This is only the second game that Cole has been to, and that was nothing compared to this time. Holden takes us in a side entrance that is for players and their families. He introduces us to the people at the family box and adds Cole and me to his family list and gets a guest pass for Brad.

The boys can barely contain themselves as Holden shows us around the empty locker room. They get to see his locker and all the indoor training equipment, the therapy room, and everything else. It's all overwhelming to them, and they just look at everything slack-jawed. When it's time for the game to start, we're walking through the tunnels to get to the elevator that takes us to the VIP box.

There's a group of us that get onto the elevator, and somehow I missed the change in the atmosphere until Holden says gruffly, "Kendall, how are you doing?"

My eyes drag from Holden to the woman he's talking to across from us. She's tall and thin with long red hair. "Hoooolden! You're here. OMG!"

She practically dives across the elevator and wraps her arms around him. He manages to turn his head before the kiss lands on his lips, but I'm not sure what's worse, seeing the woman, his ex-girlfriend-—yeah, I looked her up—plastered against Holden's body, the mark on his cheek that serves as a reminder that she kissed him, or that the fact that the pictures of the woman don't do her justice. She's absolutely breathtaking.

The fact that Holden is trying to hold the woman away from him doesn't faze her. "What are you doing here? Are you back to playing? I can't wait to see you on the field again. Do you want to get a drink after the game?"

She fires the questions to him one after another, and the longer Kendall is looking at him, the tenser I get. This is the woman that deserted him when he got injured. The one that stepped away so "he could focus on healing." It's bullshit.

I tell myself that the only reason I'm reacting is because Holden is clearly uncomfortable. He's done so much for me and Cole, and I can't just stand by and do nothing while this woman mauls him. I slide next to Holden and wrap my arms around his middle. He doesn't hesitate in bringing me snug against his body, and I put my hand on his chest. "I'm so sorry, Kimmie. He can't get a drink later. He's with me and the boys."

She looks at me. "It's Kendall."

I giggle and cover my mouth with a smile. "Oh, I'm sorry."

Her eyes narrow at me, and she looks at my hand on his chest. "Uh, Holden——"

He cuts her off as his hand slides up and down my back. "Yeah, Kendall. No drink for me. I'm busy."

"Maybe——" she starts, but Holden doesn't wait for her to respond. The elevator door opens, and he hustles me and the boys off. He doesn't give another look to Kendall, but he keeps a hold on me.

I look around, and Kendall huffs her breath and then goes in the other direction. As soon as she's out of sight, I say loudly, so Cole can hear because I don't want him to get the wrong idea, "You're welcome."

"What?" he stutters, and I pull out of his arms.

"She was all over you, and you didn't seem to be happy about it. I thought I could help, but if I assumed wrong, I'm sure you can go track her down."

I'm pointing my thumb over my shoulder where Kendall disappeared.

Holden shakes his head while Cole looks at me curiously. I shrug my shoulders. "I'm sorry, I thought I was helping."

Holden nods his head. "Uh, yeah, you were. I don't want her."

He doesn't have to say it because I know exactly what he's thinking by the intense look in his eye. He wants me.

Cole gives me a fist bump. "Good save, Mom."

I just smile and point in the direction we were moving. "So how about it, we getting to our seats? The game is about to start."

The boys run up ahead, and Holden calls out, "It's VIP Suite 6. We should be above home plate."

The boys both cheer and are speed-walking to the right door. As we walk side by side, I elbow him in the side. "You okay? Is it hard being here?"

He stops walking and turns to me. "Did you do that back there to help me?"

I start to nod, and he shakes his head. "I mean, I know you did. But is that the only reason?"

I look him in the eye and see the vulnerability

there. He's been open with me from the beginning, and it's not right for me to not do the same. My voice is soft, and I tug at the hem of my shirt anxiously. "I did it to help you… but also because I was jealous."

His eyes light up, and I swear his voice drops an octave. "You were jealous?"

I swat my hand at him, and he catches it between his. He threads our fingers together, and I know I should pull away, but I want to enjoy this feeling for just a few minutes. "Yeah, she was all over you… I didn't like it."

His lips turn up, and I suck in a breath at the way his face transforms. He pulls my hand so I'm leaning into him and whispers in my ear, "That's good because the only woman I want is you."

We're so close I can feel his breath on my cheek. All I have to do is turn my head and we could kiss. I want that more than anything, especially now after seeing the way Kendall practically mauled him. There's a rage of possession coursing through my veins, and it's making me feel impulsive and irrational. Someone walks past us, and Holden moves closer to me to let them by. My word, this man invokes things in me I thought were shriveled up and dead.

His hands go to my waist, and he dips his head to look at me. "I want to kiss you so badly right now—"

I put my hand to his chest, and it kills me to do it, but I push him away, putting some distance between us. It's a good thing I do because Cole comes out of the VIP suite. "You guys, come on, you have to see this!"

I force a smile to my face. "We're coming."

As soon as Cole disappears around the corner, I lean into Holden. "I want to kiss you too. Raincheck?"

He groans as if he's in literal pain. "Yeah, later when we're alone, all bets are off. You're going to be mine, Cat."

He walks to the open door of the suite and gestures for me to go inside. My heart is racing in my chest, and I try to forget about everything but just being here in this moment. But no matter how hard I try, I keep thinking about later, after we drop off Cole and Brad and we get to Holden's house. And I can't help but feel that tonight is going to change my life forever.

## 21

## HOLDEN

"Are you sure you don't want to watch from the dugout with your team? I mean, we're good here."

It's the third time Cat has asked, and it's clear she's worried about me. The boys have stuffed themselves full of chili dogs, popcorn, and pretzels with cheese, and they're now engrossed in the game. Cat has been looking between the field and me the whole time. "I like being here with you guys."

She gives me a doubtful look but turns back to the game. The truth is, it's freaked me out a bit on how much I've enjoyed being on this side of things. You get a different perspective from up here, and spending time with Cole and Cat has been awesome. I don't think I've ever smiled as much as I do when I'm with them.

I bring my attention back to the game and continue watching. The team has really pulled together for this one, and I take notice when I see Foreman giving instruction from his spot at shortstop. The score is seven to one, and it's the bottom of the ninth. When Carter clinches the third out, the stadium erupts with excitement. We're getting that much closer to the playoffs, and every Bears fan knows it. Cole and Brad are going crazy, and Cat is cheering at my side. I'm just smiling, arms crossed over my chest, watching my team celebrate.

Cat bumps me on the shoulder. "Go on. We're good here. Go celebrate with your team."

Fuck, she's worried about me this whole game, and I hate that. I really am okay with being up here with her. Maybe I should miss playing the game more than I do, but the fact I don't is telling. I resist putting my arm around her. "I'd rather celebrate with you."

Her cheeks turn a pretty pink, and she gestures to the field below us. "You know you're going to get back there, right?"

I give her a nod. "I know I am… with your help."

Her smile widens, and she shakes her head. "You really are a charmer, Holden Gray."

I corral the boys, and we make our way through the stadium. A few people have recognized me, but I just pull my hat down and keep my head low until we get out to the parking lot.

The boys are yawning in the backseat and are quieter now than they were on the way here.

Cat calls out to them, "Well boys, what did you think? Did you enjoy the game?"

Brad answers immediately. "It was awesome! The best game ever."

When Cole doesn't answer, Cat turns in her seat. "Cole, what about you?"

I catch his gaze in the rearview mirror, and he's looking at me instead of answering his mom. "It was good."

Cat scrunches her nose at his lackluster response but doesn't ask for him to explain. I sit up a little taller in my seat. "What is it, Cole? What are you thinking?"

He hesitates. "I dunno."

I shake my head. "No way, buddy. You're thinking of something, you can talk to me."

He avoids my gaze by looking out the window. "Well, they did better than last week."

"But?" I ask, encouraging him to tell me.

"Well… they need you out there, Holden."

I clench my hands on the steering wheel, but before I can respond, Cole continues. "I mean, of course they play better when you're out there, but since you're injured right now, they could use your voice."

I stop at a red light and turn in my seat. "My voice?"

"Yeah, they need to hear you."

The light turns green, and I pull out. We're almost to Brad's house, and I'm not understanding what Cole is saying about my voice. "What do you mean… my voice?"

He sits higher up in his seat. "Well, I'm thinking when you're on the field, you talk to your teammates. Sort of how you did tonight. You knew what was going to happen before it happened. If they had shifted like you said on that one play in the sixth inning, they would have got that out. If they'd pulled Carter from pitching when you said, they wouldn't have had that run."

I lift my shoulders in a shrug. "We don't know that."

"All I'm saying is that if you can't play… maybe you should coach."

"Cole Maples… Holden's going to play again."

Cole jerks back, and I put a hand on Cat's arm that is resting on the console. "No, it's okay."

Cole is quick to jump in. "I didn't mean it bad. I know he's going to play, but I just think he'd be a good coach… I wish he was our coach."

"Yeah," Brad chimes in. "Then maybe the coach's kid wouldn't make five errors a game."

The boys start talking about their last game, and I focus on the road in front of me. Cat keeps looking at me, and it's clear she's worried about how I'm responding to what Cole said.

As soon as we drop the boys off and are back in the car, Cat is the first one to break the silence. "You know that Cole didn't mean anything by that. You're going to play, Holden."

"I know Cole meant it as a compliment, and I know I'm going to play. Want to know what else I know?"

"What?"

I reach for her hand and thread our fingers together. "You worry too much about me. I'm not falling apart. And I one hundred percent believe I'm going to play in the playoffs, but I also know that if I didn't, I would be okay. At one time, baseball was my whole life."

"And now?" she asks in barely a whisper.

It's on the tip of my tongue to confess everything to her. To tell her that I'm getting more and more okay with not playing baseball and settling down. "I dunno, now I can see things from a different perspective. I love baseball, and I'll always be involved with it in some way, but I'm really thinking this will be my last go around on the field."

"Hmmm" is all she says, and as I pull into my driveway and turn off the car, I turn to her. "What does 'hmmm' mean?"

She opens the door and gets out, and I do the same. I walk around the truck to where she's at and reach for her hand. She grasps mine, and I pull her to me, asking again, "What does 'hmmm' mean?"

She won't look at me. "I just mean that you shouldn't make any big decisions right now. Wait until you're playing again because you might feel differently."

"But—" I start, and she shakes her head, pressing her hands to my chest.

"Holden," she says, her voice low and seductive.

I let her name roll off my tongue as I press my

hands to her lower back and hold her to me. I'm sure she can feel my hard manhood pressed against her. "Cat."

She traces her finger in circles on my chest. "Are you going to take me to bed or what?"

I take a deep breath and walk with her to the front porch. We're both silent as I unlock the front door, turn off the alarm, and reset it.

Hand in hand, we walk to the living room, and I sit down, pulling her onto my lap. She has one arm looped around my neck and the other hand is on my chest. "What are we doing here, Holden?"

She's searching my eyes, wondering why I brought her to the couch instead of the bedroom, and I want to explain it to her, but I don't think she's ready to hear it. She's convinced this is a fling, and that's not what I want. When I don't answer her fast enough, she grips my shoulders. "If you've changed your mind, Holden, you just have to tell me."

"Fuck." I grunt. "I didn't change my mind. I just thought we should talk about things first. If I take you into that bedroom, we won't be doing any talking."

She stands up and holds her hand out to me. "That's good because I'm done talking."

I stand up, but I just haul her against me. "There's a few things we need to discuss before I make you mine."

Her eyes are wide, and her breath comes out in pants. "Okay. Talk."

I smirk and pull her until our bodies are flush against each other. She fits perfectly in my arms, and I want to talk to her about forever and how I see our relationship going, but she's not ready for that talk just yet. So I tell her the one thing that I need her to agree to. "As long as we're doing this, there will be no other men… no Jeremy… no one."

She lets out a little huff. "I told you I'm not seeing him anymore."

I run my hand up her shoulder and to the back of her neck. I apply a little pressure, and she moans as she blinks her big eyes at me. "I don't share, Cat."

She looks at me stubbornly. "What about you?"

Confused, I ask her, "What about me?"

She grunts. "Right, so you want me to only be sleeping with you… no one else?"

I grit my teeth together because I don't even want to think about her with someone else. "That's right."

"And what? You can just sleep with whoever?"

She's jealous. That's the first thought that hits me, and the second is the fact that I haven't looked or even thought of another woman since I first laid eyes on Cat. "No, the only person I'll be making love to is you."

Her mouth drops. "Oh."

I bring my hand up to the side of her face and caress her cheek as I push her hair off her face. "Is that okay with you?"

She bites her lip and nods her head. "Yeah, yeah, that's okay with me."

As soon as she agrees, I'm on her. I can't hold back from kissing her another moment. Sitting next to her at the game all night, sneaking looks and touches has driven me crazy, and now that she's agreed she's mine, albeit temporarily, there's nothing stopping me.

I reach for the hem of her shirt and pull it up, parting our lips just so I can get her shirt off.

She reaches for mine and does the same. "My bed," I mumble against her lips.

She pulls away, panting. "Your bed."

I pull her through the house and don't stop until I have her standing next to my bed. I've thought about this moment for what feels like forever, and now that it's here, I don't want to fuck it up.

## 22

## CATHERINE

I can do this. I can have sex and it not mean anything.

At least that's what I'm telling myself as Holden continues to undress me. I'm holding my breath because even though he's seen my jiggly parts, I'm still unnerved by the fact I'm about to be fully naked in front of him. He kisses down my neck and across my shoulder, and when he palms my breast, my back arches, pushing me fuller into his hand.

I bite my lip to keep from groaning. This feels so damn good, and already I can feel the pull of arousal in my lower belly.

He reaches behind me, unsnapping my bra with a trained hand. *Don't say it, don't say it.* But I don't listen. "You're pretty good at that."

He pulls the silky material of my bra off my body and leans back to look at me. "What? The bra?"

Fuck, I should have kept my mouth closed. No one wants to be having sex with an insecure woman. I know he's had plenty of practice undressing women, so why did I have to bring it up? "Forget it… forget I said anything."

He's breathing hard, but he manages to get the sentence out. "You're the only one I'm thinking of right now… since the first time I saw you, you're the only woman I've thought about… the only woman I want to do this with. The past doesn't matter. All that matters is right now… Me and you."

I'm pretty sure my heart literally flips in my chest. "Charmer."

He glances down my body, then shakes his head. "Fuck, you're perfect, Cat." He cups my pussy and presses the heel of his hand against my swollen clit. "I need to see the rest of you."

I slowly kick off my shoes and take off my socks and pants and then take a deep breath and remove my underwear. I'm standing completely naked in front of him. He puts his hand on my shoulders, turns me until the back of my knees are against the bed and then gently lays me backwards.

He hovers over me, and I try to close my legs, but he stops me. "No, let me look at you."

His chest expands with every breath he takes, and his muscles ripple as he runs his hands down my inner thigh. He stops before he gets to where I need him to be, but before I let him know my frustration, he puts his hand at my core, and my whole body reacts to his touch.

He slides his finger through my slit and grunts, "Fuck, you're so pretty, Cat. You're so wet… have you been thinking about this all night?"

I couldn't lie to him if I wanted to. It's like he has me in a trance, and I nod my head.

He slides his thumb over my engorged clit, and I suck in a breath and grip the bedcover into my hands. He smiles. "I need to hear you say it, Cat. Were you thinking of this while you were sitting next to me at the ballgame tonight? Were you thinking of my mouth on you?"

I suck in air to my lungs, but it feels like I can't catch my breath. I knew he was a charmer, but I didn't know he had a degree in dirty talk. He's circling my clit and then slides his finger through my swollen slit. "Come on, Cat. Talk to me, baby.

Tell me if you've been thinking about me… about this… about us."

With my head thrown back, I can't process anything. He has me completely wound tight, and I need a release. But when he pulls his hand away, I whimper and grab on to his arm. "Yes, yes. I've thought about this… about you way before I should have."

"When?" he demands.

"Holden," I whisper because he's bringing me closer to an orgasm. "Please," I beg him.

He's pumping one finger inside me in a slow motion as he caresses my nub with his other hand. "Tell me, Cat. When?"

I lean up on my elbows to look at him. He's staring at my pussy, and his mouth is so close I can feel his hot breath on my thighs. "I wanted you since I looked at your picture in your intake folder. Before I met you, before I heard your voice, and before I ever touched you, I wanted you."

His smile is instant, and he gives my pussy a little pat. "Good girl."

I'm about to groan in frustration until he settles his big shoulders between my thighs with his face right in front of my sex. "Holden?"

"I need to taste you, Cat."

He doesn't wait for me to answer. He presses his tongue against my swollen womanhood and strokes it from my entrance to the tight bundle of nerves. My head falls back again. "Oh God."

When he sucks my clit into his mouth, I know I'm a goner. The orgasm hits me hard and fast, and my hips buck against him with uncontrolled fury. His strong arm goes across my hips to hold me in place while his tongue devours me. My whole body gets hot, and my muscles are pulled so tight that I feel like I may break any minute, and then all of a sudden, something snaps, and I let the feeling rush through me.

I thought I'd climaxed before, but this is on a whole new level. My body has no control and jerks under his touch. He laps at me, moaning as he devours my desire.

"One more," he demands.

I lift my head in shock and shake it side to side. "I can't... there's no way."

He just smiles at me. He's back to circling my clit with his finger. "That sounds like a challenge, Cat."

"No, no, it's not... I'm good... what about you?"

"Give me one more… that's what I want right now."

As I look down at him between my thighs, I take in my flushed body, erect nipples, and the beard burn on my thighs. I can still feel the aftershocks of that earth-shattering orgasm, and I really don't think I can give him what he wants. "I don't think I can."

He kisses the mound of my pussy. "Do you trust me?"

I nod. "Yes."

He turns his hand palm up and prods his finger inside me. He enters me slowly and then pulls out before repeating the pattern. I stutter, "Oh, I can't have an orgasm with penetration—Oh."

Mid-sentence, he curled his finger up and started stroking me on the inside. I've heard of the G-spot, but I've never—"Oh God," I moan.

He strokes me from the inside, and the pleasure is immense. I grab at the sheets on the bed and pull at them as he continues stroking me. When he presses down on my lower belly, there's no holding back. The orgasm takes over, and it's like I'm possessed. The sounds I make, the way my body convulses, and the pleasure is so intense it almost feels like I'm dying.

My pussy floods, and he moans before kissing me again and then moving his way up my body. When he lays his body on top of mine, I can barely open my eyes, but I feel the dig of his denim jeans against my bare skin. "You have too many clothes on," I mutter.

He laughs and rolls off me to stand next to the bed. I pry my eyelids open to watch him, and by the time he's down to his underpants, I'm on full alert. I roll to my side and watch him as he stands there with a hand on each side of his shorts, but he's not moving.

"Go ahead."

He takes a deep breath and then drops his shorts and steps out of them. I reach for him before I can even process what I'm doing. I put one finger on his tip and swipe at the precum dripping from him.

I bring my finger to my mouth to taste him, and he moans.

I smile up at him. "My turn."

I grab his hand and pull him toward me. It takes some work, but I get him to his back and lean over him. I look at his engorged manhood and back at him. He's looking at me through hooded eyes and smiling, waiting patiently. "You okay?"

I swallow and nod. "Yeah, but I feel like I should warn you… uh, I haven't done this in a long time, so uh, I feel like I should apologize—"

He cuts me off by pulling me under my arms until I'm sprawled out over top of him. "Already this has been the best experience I've ever had. If you don't want to—"

"No." I stop him. "I want to, I just don't want to disappoint you."

"You can't," he assures me.

I spread my legs so I'm straddling him and lean up. I start to move down, and his cock strokes along my core as I crawl down his body. I wrap my hand around his girth and hold on to him as I press my tongue to his tip. He moans instantly, and I do it again.

As I get more confident, I open my mouth, taking him in, letting him hit the back of my throat. I gag, but I'm not a quitter. Over and over, I take him, and as I raise my eyes to look at him, I know he's close.

## 23

## HOLDEN

She's sucking me so well I feel my balls draw up, and I'm about to blow my load. As soon as her eyes lift to mine, I know I'm a fuckin' goner. Gone in every way I can be. She's going to be mine—not just today but forever.

I strangle out the words. "Get up here, Cat."

Her eyebrows lift, but she doesn't stop. Fuck, this is too hard, but I don't want to come in her mouth, I want to come inside her pussy. I'm not sure why this is so important to me, but it is. I lift her under her arms, pulling her up my body until she's straddlling me and my seeping cock is pressed against the crevice of her ass. She wipes her mouth. "What—"

I cut her off. "I'm clean."

She leans forward, putting her hands on my chest. I'm not sure if she realizes it or not, but she's pushing her hips back and forth, grinding her pussy into my stomach. "Talk to me, baby. Tell me I can go in you bare."

"I'm clean and I'm on the pill, but…"

She stops, and I put my hands on her hips to pull her tighter against my body. She's so reactive, and she moans as she grinds into me. "Talk to me, Cat. Will you take me bare?"

She nods. "I trust you."

It's like a hit to the solar plexus, and I don't take her words lightly. "Ride me, baby."

She lifts up and wraps her hand around my length, positioning me at her entrance. She sucks in a breath as she lowers herself on me, and her whole body starts to tremble. She's tight like a vise on my dick, and I give her time to adjust to me. When she sinks a little farther, I'm concentrating on not coming right here, right now. She feels so good, and I tell her so. "Fuuuuck, You feel like you were made for me."

"I need to move, Holden."

I lean up and put my hands on her hips. "Move, baby."

She lifts up and slams back down. She twirls her

hips, finding what she likes, and it's pure torture, but I grit my teeth and take it. "That's it, Cat. Can you give me another one?"

She laughs and shakes her head. "There's no way."

I flip her to her back, lift her knees to her chest, and drive into her. She gasps and hooks her feet on my shoulders.

"Deep… you're so deep, Holden."

"Come for me, Cat."

"Arghhh." She grunts as I pummel into her.

I reach between us and press a finger to her sensitive clit. It instantly sets her off, and she clamps on to me until I have to force myself in and out.

Her head is thrown back, her whole body pulled taut, and she feels so perfect that I can't hold back another second. I let myself go and thrust into her, painting her insides until I'm spent and half out of my mind.

We're both heaving our breaths, and I'm trying to keep my weight off her, but she has her arms around me, holding me to her.

She pulls me tight to her, but I resist. "I'm going to squash you, Cat."

She doesn't release me, though; if anything, she

holds me tighter. "Please, hold me, Holden. I just need you to hold me."

I let my body sink against hers. I'm still buried inside her, but I'm not complaining. As our breaths even out, I nuzzle into her neck. "I need to get up."

I feel her chest expand as she takes a deep breath. Is there disappointment in her voice? "Okay." She releases her hold on me.

I pull out of her and then move to lie next to her. "You ready?"

Her eyes pop open, and she looks at me. "Ready for what?"

"A shower… food… and then round two?"

She leans up on her elbows. "Round two?"

I cup the side of her face. I want to tell her that this was perfect and that I want her and Cole to stay here, but I keep it to myself. "Yeah, round two, round three… whatever we can fit into tonight. And then tomorrow we're picking up Cole and—"

She half-whispers, "And then we'll be back to friends."

I chuckle and shake my head. "Oh, we're more than friends."

She puts her hand to my chest. "Holden, we agreed—"

I cover her hand with my own. "We agreed that

you want to keep this between us, and that's fine for now, but eventually—"

She cuts me off, stretching her body and then climbing over me. Her body glides across mine, and even though I'm exhausted, my cock twitches. She smiles, knowing exactly what she's doing to me. "Let's not talk about 'eventually.' Come on, Holden, if we're going to get to round three, then we better shower."

I watch her ass shake side to side as she walks to the bathroom. I give her a few seconds to herself and then follow her just in time to see her walking into the shower and standing under the hot water.

I stand at the open door and watch her. Her eyes are closed, head tilted back, and she's letting the spray hit her in the face and trail down her body. She's beautiful, and I love seeing this unguarded version of her. When she lifts her head and sees me watching her, she smiles and holds her hand out to me. "You coming in?"

I grab on to her hand like it's a lifeline and walk up to her, wrapping my arms around her. A need I've never felt before comes over me, and I hug her to me, resting my cheek on the top of her head. My arms are around her shoulders, and she lifts hers to go around my waist. But my favorite part is the way she melts into me, accepting the hug that I need from her. We stand here for so long that I worry the hot water may give out. It's been a long time since I've hugged someone, and I let all the emotions roll through me.

"You okay, Holden?" she murmurs.

I sniff. "Yeah, I'm good… the best."

She leans her head back, resting her chin on my chest, and I loosen my hold on her so I can look her in the face. "Are you okay?"

She smiles. "Yeah, I'm just surprised. I never would have thought you would be a cuddler after sex."

Hell, I'm not. I'm usually looking for ways to put some distance between me and the woman, and that's just another reason why I know what's happening between Cat and me is more than just sex. I lock my hands at her back. "I'm usually not… It's different with you."

She tenses in my arms, but I don't let her go. It's like she doesn't want to believe that this is more than it is. She has to realize this is more than just some fling. She pulls from my arms and grabs the soap off the ledge and squirts it into her hands. "Come on, Mr. Gray. Let's get you clean."

She puts her hands to my chest and starts to

wash me. I want to insist we have a real conversation, but it's clear she wants to keep this light. I'll let her have her way, for now. I cover her hands with my own. "If you're going to be running your hands over my body to get me clean, then round two is going to happen sooner rather than later."

She rolls her eyes with a big smile on her face. "Promises, promises."

And because I can't hold back any longer, I cup her face in my hands and kiss her like there's no tomorrow.

## 24

## CATHERINE

"Got it!" Cole hollers before hitting the ball. It goes over the net, straight to Chrissy.

I stand on my side of the court, knees bent, paddle ready for the ball that comes careening back at me. I hit it, and it lands in the square on the other side before bouncing out of play. "Yes!" Cole hollers, jumping up and down. "We did it, Mom!"

I'm still not sure what the rules are for pickleball, but somehow we just won a game against Chrissy and Gabe. Cole hugs me, and I soak it all in. With his arm around my waist, we walk over to the side and meet the rest of Holden's family. I'm not sure how this happened, but this morning when I finally dragged myself out of bed and said I had to shower and go get Cole, Holden convinced me to come to his family's game of pickleball.

"Having fun?" Holden asks.

Cole and Gabe are talking smack, and my cheeks are hurting from smiling so much. "I'm having a blast."

"Yeah, we always have a good time when we come."

I point around at his family. "How did you all get started playing this?"

"Well, I think Gabe and his buddies at the fire department started playing, and then Gabe started enforcing family game day once a month, so here we are."

I try not to let my jealousy show. Man, I would do anything to have this for Cole. As I look at my son and see how truly in his element he is, I know he would flourish with a big family like this. "Well, it's fun."

Holden gives me a look, and he doesn't have to say a word for me to know what he's thinking. It's probably the same thing I've thought about all morning. Last night was perfect. The sex was out of this world, but it's more than that. We laughed, we talked, we held each other. It didn't feel like a fling. But just as soon as my mind starts to go to that thought, I know I need to quit thinking that way. Holden is a professional baseball player, and as soon as he's back to playing, this will be nothing but a distant memory for him.

I'm drawn from my thoughts when King holds up his paddle. "All right, me and Haven against Dom and Cole."

Haven calls out, rubbing her round belly. "Take it easy on me, I'm carrying an extra person here."

"I'm going to run to the ladies room," I tell Holden.

"I'll go with you."

I stop him, holding up my hand. "No, it's fine. It's just right there, I'll be right back."

I walk away, and the whole way across the park, I try to get my thoughts in order. I keep reminding myself that I can do this. I can do a fling without my heart getting involved.

I finally reach the bathroom, and after taking care of business, I stare at myself in the mirror as I wash my hands. There's a light in my eyes that hasn't been there in a long time. I make a promise to myself that even when this is over, I'm going to do everything I possibly can to keep that light burning bright.

After drying my hands, I'm walking out of the

bathroom and come to a halt when I see Holden leaning up against the column. "Hey."

He pulls me toward him, spins me until my back is against the column, and then leans into me until our bodies are flush against each other. I barely have time to catch my breath and he's kissing me. It's heady to feel his erection against my belly. I should be worrying about who's going to see us, but I let myself fall deep into the kiss.

I pull away, breathless. "Someone is going to see us."

It doesn't faze him that I've pulled my mouth away because he starts kissing my neck. "I don't care," he mutters.

He palms my breast through my thin shirt, and I moan. "Holden."

"Gabe, I can go to the restrooms by myself, I don't need a chaperone!" Chrissy says almost angrily. I gasp at the thought of getting caught, but Holden grabs me, pulling me to the side of the building away from Chrissy and Gabe.

"That's tough, Chrissy. You can never be too safe," Gabe says easily.

"This is Whiskey Run!" she exclaims.

I lean my head against the concrete wall. This is it. We're going to get caught. Chrissy and Gabe and then the rest of the family are going to know what's going on here… and then Cole, oh my God, Cole.

Holden is clueless to my internal freakout because he has me plastered to him in a hug, stroking my hair as he holds on to me.

The door to the bathroom squeaks, and I hear Chrissy say, "You going to follow me in here or are you going to let me pee on my own?" There's a pause and then Chrissy sounds exasperated. "Gabe! What are you doing?"

Silence and then a gruff Gabe says, "It's all clear, go on in. I'll be here waiting for you."

More silence and then a stunned Chrissy says, "Did you really just check the bathroom to see if it was empty?"

"You can't be too careful," Gabe answers her.

The door closes, and there is silence. I'm holding my breath, hoping that Gabe doesn't come around the corner and see us.

A few minutes pass by, and the bathroom door opens and Chrissy and Gabe argue as they walk away.

As soon as they're gone, I struggle out of Holden's arms. I point at him. "We can't keep doing this. You agreed to keep this between us."

"About that…" Holden starts, and I'm shaking

my head at him. I start walking toward the pickleball courts, and he catches up to me. "I don't want to hide this anymore."

I blurt out a laugh and throw my hands in the air. "Really? One night together and you want to change everything?"

Holden grabs my hand and pulls me to a stop. "Cat, you know last night was—"

I stop him before he says anything. I know what he's going to say, and he's right. I've never felt what I felt last night, but that doesn't mean I can put all my faith into him because I had great sex.

"This is it, Holden. Take it or leave it. We keep this between the two of us or it's over."

His mouth drops, and he shakes his head. He's mad, and he leans toward me. "Ending this is not an option, Catherine."

Why is he acting like this is important to him? I've heard the stories about him and how he's a player; I've seen the pictures online of him with different women. He's acting like I'm special to him, but I know I'm not. "What part of a fling do you not get, Holden? That's all this is."

Before he can say anything else, I walk away from him and into the fenced-in area of the courts. Chrissy waves at me. "Where have you been?"

"I got sidetracked. This park is beautiful, isn't it?"

Chrissy is nodding her head in agreement, but I don't miss the question on her face. Holden walks up behind me, and Chrissy frowns at him. "Holden, it's okay. You're going to get to play soon."

Gabe, Cole, King, and Haven all walk off the court. "We won, Mom!" Cole says, running toward me.

I hold my fist up. "Good job, son."

King is huffing and puffing. "Yeah, your son is a natural."

Cole's chest expands as he smiles proudly up at King. Dom ruffles his hair. "Yeah, little dude, you can be my partner any time."

Cole looks between Dom and King, and I swear he looks like he's going to explode from happiness.

I hate to end this, but it's time for us to go. Now more than ever, I have to remind myself that this is not our family. "Well, we appreciate you all letting us join you, but we better get going."

Chrissy gasps. "What? No way. You can't leave now. We're all going to eat at Red's Diner. It's tradition, you have to go."

Before I can decline, Cole is jumping up and down. "Mom, please, can we go?"

It's on the tip of my tongue to say no, but Cole looks so hopeful I don't have the heart to say it. I loop my arm around his neck and look around at Holden's family. They're all looking at me expectantly. I glance at Holden, and he nods his head at me. "Okay, if you're sure we won't be intruding."

Dom comes over and puts one arm around me. "Intruding? No way. We want you to come… right, Holden?"

Holden looks at his brother and growls. "Yeah, we do."

Dom has a huge smirk on his face when he says to me, "And you and Cole can ride with me."

Holden looks as if he's about to rip Dom's arm off his shoulder, but his voice is very steady. "They came here with me. They're going home with me so they're going to ride with me."

Even though Holden is holding himself tensely, he smiles when he looks at me. "You ready to go?"

I nod. "Come on, Cole. See you at the restaurant, everyone."

They all say bye as we walk the different directions to our cars.

Cole runs up ahead of us as Holden falls into step beside me. "I wasn't even thinking about the fact that we rode here together. I should have driven separately so you could have enjoyed lunch with your family."

He blows out a breath and seems frustrated. "I like being with you and Cole. Why do you find that so hard to believe, Cat?"

With my head down, I mutter, "Because my ex, Cole's father, walked out on us without a second glance, and I promised myself that I would never put him, put myself, through that again."

"So this is not about me or because you think I'm some kind of player… this is about you and your fears."

"Does it really matter, Holden? This is all this can be. We're from two very different worlds, and once you get back to your real life, you'll realize it."

He opens his mouth just as Cole hollers from the side of the truck, "Hey, Mom, can I get a piece of the cinnamon apple Blaze cake?"

I pick up my pace because being alone with Holden makes me want things I know I can't have. "Yeah, and you know what? I think I'll get me a piece too."

Holden gets into the driver's side of the truck, and Cole asks him, "What about you, Holden? You getting a piece of the cinnamon apple cake?"

He shrugs. "I'll snag a bite from someone, but my boss says I'm training and gotta watch my sugar."

Cole seems to think about it. "Why don't we get one piece of cake and all three of us can share it together?"

I agree with Cole. "That's a good idea, let's do that."

Holden turns in his seat and gives Cole a long look and then does the same to me. The way he stares at me hits me right in the chest. It's a look of longing and wanting to belong, and even though Cole just offered to share cake with him, it seems like it means so much more. "I like that idea," he mutters, his voice thick with emotion.

I want to reach for him and hold his hand. I want to tell him that I like spending time with him and give him everything he wants just so that sad look on his face will go away, but I don't do any of that. I can't. My son is already so attached to him that he's going to be sad when we return to our home on the other side of town. I'm already grieving that the "fling" is running out of time. I remind myself again that this is temporary and force a smile to my face and then look out the window as Holden drives us across town.

## 25

HOLDEN

It's been two days since I've had Cat in my arms, and I miss her. She's determined to keep things on the up and up when we're doing therapy, and we haven't had any extra alone time. The need to talk to her is intense.

I stare up at the ceiling of my bedroom, debating what I should do. Fuck it, what have I got to lose?

I pick up my phone off the bedside table. I take a deep breath and text her. "Hey."

I roll my eyes as soon as I hit send. *Real smooth, Gray.*

She texts back almost immediately. "Hey."

Encouraged that she didn't just leave me on read, I reply, "I want to see you."

My phone lights up with her reply. "You saw me all day."

I lean up. "Are you coming to me or am I coming to you?"

The dots pop up that she's typing, and then she stops. I type out really quick. "Don't think about it. Just come to me, Cat."

The dots never come back, and I'm about to stomp down the hallway when I hear a small knock on my door. I'm out of my bed and across the room like the speed of light. I pull the door open and gape at her. She's smiling up at me, and it's so good to see her smile that I pull her against me and kiss her like it's my last dying breath.

She moans softly, pulling away. "The door... Cole..."

I shut the door and then draw her back into my arms. Her hands are everywhere, and I grab her arms to hold her in place. "We need to talk."

"We've talked enough, Holden. Please, we have less than a month together, can we just enjoy it?"

"But—" I start and then stop when she pulls off her tank top, and her breasts are bared to me. It's like all the blood rushes south and I forget what I was even going to say. She pushes me, and I easily fall backwards on the bed. She takes off her panties and shorts in one swoop and then dips her hands into each side of my underwear and pulls them down my hips and legs. My cock twitches as she climbs up to straddle me.

She doesn't waste any time as she wraps her hand around my girth and positions me at her entrance. She slowly slides down my length, and it's only when she's fully seated that she lets out a long, satisfied breath.

She rocks back and forth, and I lean up, circling my arms around her back as I thrust into her. Her head has fallen back and her eyes are clenched closed. I'm so close already, but I refuse to let her make this just some booty call.

"Look at me, Cat."

She shakes her head, and her hands go to my shoulders as she grinds into me.

"Dammit, look at me," I whisper harshly.

She lifts her head and looks at me with a challenge.

"Look at me, Cat. I just want to look into your eyes while you use me to get off."

She gasps. "I'm not using you."

She puts her hands on my cheek and searches my face. "I'm not using you, Holden."

I want to talk to her and tell her how I feel, but

she doesn't want to hear it, so I appease myself by looking into her eyes as I drive into her.

I pull her hips up a little and hit her at a different angle. She groans, and her eyes start to drift closed. "Oh God."

"No, look at me, baby. I want to see your pretty blues when you come."

She pulls me tighter and stares into my eyes as she rides me. "It feels sooo good, Holden."

"Yeah, baby. So good."

She's so close. I can feel the tiny spasm of her pussy walls, and her channel is slick and heated. She comes undone in my arms with her pupils huge in her eyes, but she never looks away. There's so much emotion between us, and seeing the way she's looking at me takes my orgasm to another level. I've never come looking into a woman's eyes, and I'll never do it again unless I'm with Cat.

I keep thrusting, and she matches my pace. When we're both spent, she rests her head on my shoulder, and I stroke her hair. She's breathless. "Holden."

"Yeah, baby?"

She lifts her head. "I'm not using you. I wouldn't do that."

"I know that… "

"I just…" she starts, but she buries her head in my neck and stops talking.

I hold her to me. "It's okay."

She takes a deep breath. "I should go back to my room."

"Stay," I demand. "Just lie here with me and let me hold you for a while."

She's going to say no. I can feel the way her body tenses that she's going to tell me no, but she surprises me with a whispered "Okay."

I lift her from my body and lay her back on the bed. She's limp, and she lies there with her arm over her head. I go to the bathroom and turn on the water in the sink. As soon as it warms up, I wet a washcloth and make my way back to Cat. I tenderly clean her up, and she's so out of it, she just lets me.

"Cat, honey, you okay?"

"Mmm hmmm," she says with a small smile on her face.

I chuckle, go to clean myself up, and then make my way back to the bed. I climb in next to her, tuck her against my body, and pull the blankets up over us.

She burrows into me, and I hold her so tightly she laughs and pulls back a little.

"Sorry." I stroke her hair. "Cat?"

She yawns. "Yeah?"

"Can I ask you about Cole's dad?"

She tenses, and I rub my hand up and down her back. "Forget it, if you don't want to talk about it—"

She shakes her head. "No, it's fine. It was a long time ago. Cole was just a few months old when he moved away."

"He just moved away?"

She nods against my chest. "Yeah, he didn't want to be a dad."

"Umph, okay, so he didn't want to be a dad. He just left?"

"Yep, and we haven't heard from him since."

I raise up so I can see her face. "He hasn't reached out to Cole at all? Sent you money? Checked on him? Anything?"

She shakes her head. "It's his loss."

I hold her a little tighter. "Fuck yeah, it's his loss."

"I was fine with him leaving. He was cheating on me, and it was a bad situation, and even though I know Cole needed a man in his life, I do think he was better off without Mike's influence. It's been hard, playing the role of mom and dad, and heck, Cole's probably going to need therapy someday—"

I lift her chin so she's looking at me. "You've done a great job with him, Cat. He's a great young man. He's smart, caring, kind, he works hard, he's determined. I think he's going to do great in life."

She lets out a shuddered breath. "Thank you. It's nice to hear that because a lot of times I just hear the things in my head, and I feel like I'm screwing up every day… multiple times a day."

"You're a good mother… the best."

I start stroking her hair again. "So that must have been hard, single mom and all that. Were your parents supportive?"

"Yeah, they were."

"But?" I ask her, hearing the hesitancy in her voice.

"No, they were supportive, but my parents were older when they had me. When Cole was around seven years old, they retired to Florida. We see them around once a year, but it's fine."

"So you're doing this all on your own?"

She shrugs. "Well, me and Cole, but it's fine."

I want to tell her that I'm here for her and that I won't walk away, but she'd either laugh in my face or she'd freak out and leave. She doesn't believe me when I tell her I want more than a fling, and it's crazy to think that I would give it all up—the career, the traveling, all of it, if I had her and Cole in my life.

We end up talking through the night, and just before dawn, I take her again because even though I can't tell her, I try and show her how I feel about her. Somehow I have to break through the walls she's built around her heart.

## 26

## CATHERINE

It's been a whirlwind of a day. Heck, it's been a whirlwind of a month, but we did it. Well, Holden did it. He's made it back to play in the playoffs. The team doctor did a final examination yesterday, and Holden has been approved to play in the game today.

It's a big occasion, and we're all here to celebrate it. Holden tried to get us all in a VIP box, but I wanted to sit in the stands, and then his whole family decided they wanted the same. So here Cole and I sit, surrounded by Holden's family, and I've never felt so happy, excited, and nervous in my life.

Chrissy leans over and nudges me with her shoulder. "He's going to be fine."

"I know. He's going to be great," I tell her, and I truly believe that too.

"There he is!" Cole stands up and points toward the dugout. He's in full gear in his shin guards and chest protector, and he's walking to the mound with his glove in one hand and his face guard in his other. He talks to the pitcher, they slap gloves, and then as he's walking to home plate to get into position, he raises his head and stares straight at me. He winks, and I can feel my whole body get hot. This last month we've spent so much time together, and my heart is already breaking, knowing that it's all coming to an end.

"Well, well, well," Chrissy says, turning in her seat and staring at me.

Shit. She saw the wink, but I play dumb. "What is it?"

"You and my brother," she says loudly.

I guess I'm not good at playing dumb because I "shhhh" her real loud. "Chrissy, I don't know what you're talking about."

She throws her arm around my shoulder. "Well, I'll just say that Haven and I would be happy to have another sister in the family. We are still outnumbered by all the boys."

Her nose is scrunched up when she says *boys*,

and I would laugh if I wasn't having an inner freakout. "It's not like that."

She laughs. "Oh, trust me. I know Holden, and I've never seen him like this before. It's like that."

I let my gaze go back to where Holden stands, and I can't think too hard on what Chrissy says because the pitcher is finished warming up, and the game is starting.

I'm on the edge of my seat the whole game. Even Cole is hooked because he doesn't get up once for food or candy.

By the end of the game—the Bears win—it's been a rollercoaster of an evening, and I feel physically and mentally exhausted.

Holden ended up hitting two home runs and made a huge play at home. I've watched him closely, hoping he wouldn't have any pain, and it appears he's feeling good.

After the team gives celebratory high-fives, Holden points at me in the stand for us to come down. "Uh, I think Holden wants us to come down to the field."

Chrissy just laughs. "Uh, he doesn't want us down there. He's pointing at you and Cole."

I nod. "Right, well, I want to check on how his arm is feeling anyway."

Chrissy just gives me a knowing nod and practically shoves me out of the aisle. Cole and I walk toward the fence, and a security guard is standing at the gate. Holden runs over to us. "Charlie, they're with me."

The security guard nods his head. "Good job tonight, Holden. Glad to see you back."

He opens the gate and waves me and Cole through.

Holden pulls Cole and me into a hug, and I'm tense, fighting not to melt into his hold. I pull back and awkwardly pat him on the shoulder. "Good game, Holden."

Cole is staring up at Holden like he hung the moon. "It was a great game, Holden."

He scruffs Cole's hair. "Thanks, bud."

"So how do you feel? Any pain? Tightness?"

He laughs and rolls his shoulder. "I feel great, and don't worry, the trainer already said he's meeting me in the therapy room to do some recovery on my arm."

"Great." I pull Cole toward me. "Well, we'll get out of your hair. It's been great working with you, Holden, and—"

He cuts me off. "I'll see you at home later and—"

I blurt out without even thinking. "I moved our stuff back home."

His mouth drops open. "You what?"

And at the same time, Cole turns to look at me in surprise. "Mom!"

I look Cole in his face, and I feel like crap that I'm putting him through this. I should have never put him in this position to have his heart broken. "Son, we knew this was temporary."

He's shaking his head in disbelief. "But I thought…"

Holden puts his hand on Cole's shoulder. "Cole, why don't you go talk to Carter. I talked to him about showing you his slider."

"Really?"

Holden smiles, but it doesn't reach his eyes. "Yeah, go check it out. It really moves when he throws it."

Cole walks over to Carter, and Holden gives them a nod before turning back at me. "What are you doing, Cat?"

I jut my chin at him defiantly.

His gaze softens. "Why are you doing this?"

I cross my arms over my chest and tell myself that I'm not going to cry. I'm trying to appear tough and in control, but I'm spiraling. "Because we both knew this was coming. This was temporary… a fling." I take a step back. "And it's over."

He's staring at me in shock. Everyone is laughing and having a good time around us, and I've completely ruined his night for him. "Look, go celebrate with your team. This is huge, Holden. You're back. You're in the playoffs."

He steps toward me, and his voice is low. "I was there, Cat. This was more than a fling, and you know it. You're scared, that's all. You're scared, and you're running away."

I give him a dismissive wave of my hand. "I'm not running away. We agreed—"

He's angry and barely able to contain himself. He's gritting his teeth. "I agreed to keep this between us until we were no longer working together. I didn't agree that this was a fling or something temporary."

I can't take much more of this. He could easily wear me down, but I have to remind myself that in the long run, this is for the best. "Stop. It's over, Holden. You and I are done."

His mouth drops at the same time Cole comes back over to where we're standing. "You guys okay? Because everyone is watching you."

I force a smile to my face. "Of course, everything is okay. Tell Holden bye, honey."

Cole wants to argue with me, but he can either tell I'm barely holding on here or he knows that now is not a good time to disagree with me. "Bye, Holden. I have a game tomorrow so won't be able to watch you play, but good luck. I hope you win."

Holden grips him on the shoulder. "Good luck at your game tomorrow. Just go out there and do your thing. Don't get too into your head and you got this."

Cole is biting his lip, but he nods his head. "Okay."

I put my arm around my son's shoulder. "Bye, Holden. Thank you for... everything."

He crosses his arms over his chest. "I'll talk to you soon."

As Cole and I walk away, Holden's family is watching us. I hold my hand up and wave at them as we go in the opposite direction. I should go talk to them, but I don't have the strength to do it. No, it's for the best to get a clean cut and just end it.

Neither Cole and I say a word the whole walk to the car. It's not until we're crossing the city limits into Whiskey Run that Cole asks, "You okay, Mom?"

It takes everything in me, but I force a happy tone. "Of course. You doing okay?"

Instead of answering, he looks out the window.

I reach over and elbow him lightly. "Hey, buddy, you okay?"

He shrugs, still not looking at me. "I just thought…"

His voice trails off, and I grip the steering wheel a little tighter. "You thought what?"

He shakes his head. "Nothing. Do you think we'll ever see Holden again, Mom?"

"Yeah, honey. He's got a lot going on right now, but we live in the same town. I'm sure we'll see him sometime."

It's clear my answer doesn't make him any happier. I'm kicking myself for getting him into this, but who would have thought this would happen? I wouldn't have thought Cole would get so attached so quickly. And who would have thought that I'd fall in love with my patient? Sure as hell not me.

## HOLDEN

I know she's not here, but I keep looking in the stands for her, and every time I don't see her big blue eyes and long blond hair, I get more upset about the whole situation. She's scared. I know she is, and somehow I have to prove to her that I'm along for the whole ride. I don't plan on abandoning her or her son.

We're up to bat, and I'm standing on third. If Carter can hit the ball on the ground somewhere, I can make it home and tie it up. I have a big lead, and I'm hoping for a passed ball, a hit, a homerun or anything. With two outs, I'm running on anything.

Carter hits the ball, and I take off running to

home plate as fast as I can. The ball goes straight to the pitcher, and he catches it, getting Carter out.

I stop running and shake my head. If we'd won, it would have been over. We would have ended the season as champions, but in a series of best two out of three, we now have to play again tomorrow.

I look up in the stands where my brother was minutes ago, and see he's already gone. It felt good being back last night, but now I realize that a lot of it was knowing Cat and Cole were in the stands. Today was different.

When I make it back to my locker, I grab my phone to call my brother. "Gabe, what's up? I saw you up in the stands, you still here?"

"No man, sorry. I didn't stick around. I'll be at the game tomorrow. We're all coming."

"Sounds good, man. Thanks for coming."

There's a car horn and then Gabe keeps talking. "Yeah, I would have stuck around, but I'm trying to make it to Cole's game. King said the umpires were late getting there, so I should still be able to make it."

"The game is still playing?"

"Yeah, it's like top of the fourth. You could still make it if you wanted to."

"I'll be there."

I don't waste any time with a shower. I put on some deodorant, shorts, and a T-shirt and then go to explain to my coach why I need to go. He gives me shit, but I don't back down, and within fifteen minutes, I'm on the road back to Whiskey Run. I drive faster than I should, and when I get there, it's the top of the seventh.

I stand out in the outfield and look for Cole, finding him on first base. Then I look for Cat and see her sitting in the stands next to some man I don't know and surrounded by my family.

My chest expands a little as I see my family surrounding Cat. They know what her and her son mean to me, and it means a lot to me that they're here when I couldn't be.

I watch the rest of the game standing in the outfield, and when Cole wins the game with a walk-off homerun, I'm hollering from the outfield as my family and Cat go crazy in the stands. Even though I feel like my world is falling apart, I'm still happy for Cole. He deserves this.

I'm beaming as I watch his team dogpile him.

I completely miss my brother, Dom, approaching me. "Sorry about the game."

I shake my head, still smiling for Cole. "It's all good. We'll get them tomorrow."

Dom stops next to me and gestures to the stands. "Don't you think you should go over there?"

I look at Cat talking to the man beside her, and my hands form into fists. I've never wanted to punch a man that I don't know more than I do now. "Why? It looks like she's already moved on."

Dom just nods his head. "So there was something going on with you two."

I shrug and can't keep the anger out of my voice. "Ask her. She'll tell you it was just a fling."

Dom just shakes his head. "Well, well, well. It finally happened. The mighty Holden Gray has fallen in love."

I don't even bother trying to deny it. "Yeah, and she wants nothing to do with me."

"Hmmm," Dom says. "That's funny, because Chrissy was telling me that Cat was watching your game on her phone through her son's game. That doesn't sound like a woman that has moved on."

I look at Cat, and she's getting up from the bleachers, walking to the field with the other parents, and that same guy is glued to her side. Who the fuck is he, anyway? When he offers his arm to help her descend the stairs, my heart starts to race. I should be the one helping her, not this bozo.

"Holden, are you listening to me? Look, it's obvious to all of us that you love the girl and we all decided that she and Cole fit perfectly in with our family and we're not letting you fuck this up."

I grip the fence in front of me, and my knuckles turn white. "Fuck, Dom, I don't know what you want me to do. She wanted a fling—"

He grips my shoulder. "Make her want more."

I let his words sink in, and I'm trying to figure out what's going on. The boys are all on the field, and the men are all joining them. There are a couple of moms, Cat included, that walk out there, gloves in hand. What the fuck is going on?

"About time you showed up. You going to save Cat?"

I'm so focused on what Cat is doing that I didn't even see Chrissy walking toward us. "Save her from what?"

"Well, first of all, whoever the guy sitting next to her is. He's not taking a hint, and King had to tell him hands off at one point. Secondly, I guess it's tradition to play a father/son game after the last season game."

I don't even think about it. I grip the fence and jump over it. As I walk in from the outfield, I'm heading straight for Cat. That guy is still standing next to her, and it takes everything in me not to tackle him. I stop next to Cat, between her and the guy.

She doesn't seem surprised to see me. "Hey, I'm sorry about the game."

I shrug. "It's okay. We'll get them tomorrow." I point to where the boys are standing with their coach. "You care if I do the honors?"

"Your shoulder—" she starts.

I shake my head. "My shoulder is fine."

She shrugs. "Cole would love that. Do you have a glove with you?"

I point at the pink glove she's holding. "Can I borrow yours?"

She holds up the glove with a smirk. "You're going to use a pink glove?"

I shrug again. "If it means I get to play with Cole, I will."

Her smile is instant, and she nods. "Yeah, he would love that. He's already missing you."

I lean my head down and search her eyes. "What about you? Have you missed me?"

She doesn't think about it, she doesn't blink, nothing. "Yes, I've missed you too."

It's like a weight has been lifted off my shoulders. "All right, I'll be back." I turn to look at the man standing next to me. "You ready to play?"

He looks at Cat, but she doesn't even notice because she's looking at me with her heart in her eyes. I can't resist her, so I lean down and kiss her on the forehead before walking up to where Cole is, bringing the other man with me. "Find your son," I say before leaving him.

Cole's eyes are huge as he looks up at me. "Holden, what? Your game?"

I put my arm around his shoulders, and he leans into me. "We lost, but we'll get another chance tomorrow. I hope you and your mom will come to it. I think you two are my lucky charms."

He nods his head. "Yeah, yeah, that would be awesome."

I gesture to the field. "So I borrowed your mom's glove. Is it okay if I play?"

His mouth drops. "You want to play with us?"

I chuckle. "Yeah, is that okay?"

All of a sudden, all Cole's teammates are begging to be on his team. The coach has to divvy up the teams, and it doesn't go unnoticed that he puts himself and his son on our team.

And for the next hour, I have the time of my life.

## 28

## CATHERINE

As soon as I see Cole is happy about Holden switching places with me, I make my way off the field and go back to sitting in the stands with Holden's family. "Sitting this one out?" Chrissy asks.

She's smirking at me, and I shrug my shoulders. "Yeah."

She leans forward and squints. "Wow, I can see Cole's and Holden's smiles from here."

I swallow and nod. "Yeah, they both seem pretty pleased."

Chrissy turns in her seat. "What about you, Cat? You deserve happiness too."

I choke back the emotion, cover my heart with my palm, and watch the game taking place in front of me. All I can do is watch the way Cole laughs at something Holden says to him and the way they encourage each other. Holden doesn't look like a man that just lost a big game. If anything, he looks like a man that is completely happy with his life right now.

They only play a few innings, and even though Holden's family all stays to watch, I am glued to the game instead of the conversation around me.

I reflect on the last twenty-four hours and how I have really missed Holden. I'm not sure what to make of him being here tonight, but I'm not going to let this opportunity pass me by. The future is unknown, but I know I'll regret it for the rest of my life if I don't at least tell him how I feel.

When the game is over, I watch as Holden carries that pink glove in one hand with his other arm around Cole. They're talking and laughing, and they stop a few times as people come up to fist-bump them and congratulate them on the game.

When they step off the field, Holden looks up and watches me until he and Cole stop in front of me. "Good game, guys."

Cole is looking between me and Holden. "Thanks, Mom. I'm going to hang out with Gabe and King so you guys can talk."

I nod as I look at Holden, trying to read what he's thinking. I suck in a deep breath and try to calm my nerves. "Do you have a few minutes to talk?"

He nods, but the parents keep stopping to talk to us until finally, Holden holds his hand out to me, and as soon as I put my hand in his, he's pulling me toward the outfield. We only stop when King hollers out to us, "We're taking Cole for ice cream. You can pick him up at the house later."

Holden looks at me. "Is that okay with you?"

I nod, and Holden waves them off.

Once we're in the parking lot, Holden stops next to his truck and shoves his hand through his hair. "Do you like me, Cat? Do you like being with me?"

I shake my head side to side. "No... I mean yes."

Holden sucks in a breath. "Which is it, because you're killing me here."

I pull back my shoulders and tilt my head back so I'm looking him straight in the face. "Holden, I like being with you because usually my mind goes a hundred miles a minute, but with you, it's like there's a calm that comes over me."

Before he can say anything, I take a step toward

him and put my hands at his waist. He sucks in a breath on contact, but he doesn't reach for me, and I can't say I blame him. I've been hot and cold, and he deserves more than that. "I like that you make me laugh. I like that you're good to my son. I like that you care about your family. But no, Holden. I don't like you." I shudder a breath and force the words out. "I'm falling in love with you. I love being with you, and it scares the hell out of me."

His hands go to my shoulders. "Why?"

I lift my shoulders up. "Look at your life. I can't compete with that."

He blurts out a laugh. "You don't get it, Cat. You want to know what I was thinking about at my game tonight?"

I blink at him, scared to ask, but I have to know. "What?"

"You. None of it mattered since you and Cole weren't there. I know it seems like this all happened so fast, but it feels like forever that I've been waiting for you. I love you, Cat, and I know that scares you, but I can't do the secret thing anymore. I want the world to know you're mine."

I'm trembling, but I'm not going to let my fear hold me back. "I love you too, Holden."

He wastes no time. He pulls me flush against his body and kisses me until I'm breathless. The only reason we pull apart is because there's clapping, and when we lift our heads to look, we see King, Haven, and Cole all sitting in King's car. King leans out the window. "See you later."

Holden twirls my hair in his fingers. "I talked to Cole out there tonight. I asked him if he was okay with us dating."

I bite my lip and try to contain my smile. How is this my life? "I don't even have to ask what he said. I'm sure he said he was happy about it."

Holden presses his finger to my lip and soothes across where I was biting it. "Yeah, but he told me that if I was serious about you that I should think about marrying you."

I can feel all the heat rush to my face. "Oh my God, he didn't."

He's chuckling. "He did. Does that freak you out?"

I'm surprised by his question, but instead of answering him, I ask him the same thing in return. "What about you? Does that freak you out?"

He cradles my face in his hands. "No, I told him I'd see if I could talk you into it."

Speechless, all I can do is stare at him.

He doesn't blink, look away, or hesitate. "I'm going to get you used to the idea of us being together, but eventually, you're going to be Mrs. Catherine Gray."

"Oh, Holden."

He pulls me in for another kiss, and before I get too carried away, he pulls back. "I'm sorry, but I have to go back to Jasper tonight. Let's go get Cole and let me get you two home."

"I'll go get him so you can get back. I'm going to come to the game tomorrow, if that's okay."

His eyes light up. "Okay? Of course it's okay. I want you both there. I'll leave you tickets at the gate."

I grasp his hand. "Walk me to my car."

Hand in hand, we walk. "This doesn't feel right. I want to be with you tonight."

"Your last game of the season is tomorrow, Holden. We can be together after that. I mean, you may want to celebrate or do something else tomorrow night, but we can be together another day."

He stops walking. "You don't get it. I want to be with you… I win, I lose, whatever. I want to be with you."

I go up on my tiptoes. "I want that too."

We kiss again, and my heart does a little flutter in my chest. Holden makes me feel things I've never felt before, and even though it scares me, I'm going in full force. No more hiding, no more fear, I'm going to love Holden for as long as he'll let me.

## 29

## HOLDEN

I can't help it. I keep looking up into the stands where my family and Cat and Cole are sitting. As soon as Cat and Cole showed up, it's like I knew they were here. And when I saw that she was wearing my jersey, it took everything in me not to run up the stands where she's sitting.

It's the bottom of the ninth, and it's a tied ballgame. I should be concentrating on the game, but instead, I'm standing at the edge of the dugout, wondering how I'm going to get through the crowd to Cat when the game is over.

"Gray, you're up."

I pull my eyes off Cat, grab my bat, and make my way to home plate. If I want to get to my girl and claim her in front of everybody, I need to take control of things.

I stand at the plate, ready to hit, and watch the first ball go by. "Strike."

I stay in the box, bat over my shoulder as another pitch comes. "Strike," the umpire calls.

If I don't do something, we're going into extra innings, and I'm ready for this game to be over. I kick my feet in the dirt, crowd the plate, and choke up on the bat. I watch as the pitcher wipes his brow and then gears up to throw the ball.

The ball is coming in fast, and I swing like my life depends on it.

As soon as the ball leaves the bat, I know it's going over. Normally, I'd jog around the bases, but I'm a man on a mission.

I'm running, giving it all I got, and as I cross home plate, I just keep going. My team all runs to the middle of the field, but I head off into the stands, and straight to Cat. She has her arms wide open, waiting for me, and I pick her up, twirling her around. She receives me way better than I ever would have dreamed, but she leans down to kiss me, and I take over from there. The crowd is thunderous around us, and my brothers and sister are all crowding us. I pull Cat under my arm and

Cole against my other side to hug them both to me. I bury my head into the top of Cat's hair and breathe her in. Never in my life have I been happier than I am in this moment. Not because of a game, but because of the two people in my arms right now.

"Wait for me, okay? I'm going to go shower and see the guys."

Cat nods. "Yeah, we rode here with King."

I pull her to me for another hug. "And you'll leave with me."

After hugging the rest of my family, I make my way back to the field. I've thought about this all day, and I know what I want to do.

When we finally make it to the locker room, I talk to my coach first, then my team. After a quick shower, I make my way out to the concourse to find Cat and Cole.

They're both all smiles when they see me, and I hold hands with Cat as we walk out to my truck. We're almost to Whiskey Run, and I know I need to tell them both what I did tonight.

"There's something I need to tell you two."

Cat and I are holding hands, and they're resting on the console between us. She squeezes mine a little tighter. "What is it?"

Cole leans up as much as his seatbelt will let him, and I meet his gaze in the rearview mirror. My only hesitancy is him. I hope he's not disappointed in me when I tell him. "I told my coach and my team that today was my last game. I'm officially retiring."

Cat turns in her seat and looks at me with wide eyes. "Oh, Holden."

I shake my head, not wanting her to worry. "I'm happy with my decision. It's what I want." As soon as I see the acceptance on her face and I get to a stop sign, I turn to Cole. "You okay, bud?"

He's looking out the window. "What does this mean?"

Patiently, I explain to him, "Well, I won't be playing for the Jasper Bears anymore. Coach McGuire wants to talk to me about coaching, but that's something I'll have to think about. I don't know if I want to travel anymore."

"If you're not playing, does that mean that you'll be around more? That I'd get to see you more?"

I choke up at the question. "Would you like that?"

Finally, he turns his head away from the window and looks at me. There's so much longing on his face, I make a promise right then and there that I'm going to always be there for him. It's almost a whisper, but I hear him say, "Yeah, I would."

I'm too overcome with emotion to say anything, so I just nod my head, and after looking both ways, I push on the gas.

Everyone is silent the rest of the way home, and when we get to my house, I park the truck and walk up to the front door with them.

Cole is all smiles, but Cat is more reserved. "Holden, what are we doing here?"

"Well, I thought we should talk. Is that okay?"

Her interest piqued, she nods her head, and I lead them to the living room. They both sit down on the couch, and I sit on the coffee table in front of them. I decide not to beat around the bush. "I want you guys to move in here."

"What?" Cat asks as Cole pumps his fist in the air. "Yes!"

"Holden, we can't do that."

"Why not?" I ask her, ready to argue any excuse she can give me.

"Well, because…" She looks at Cole and then raises her eyebrows at me. "Holden, it wouldn't be appropriate."

I nod knowingly. "For now, you would be in

your old rooms, but I want you both here, under my roof, with me." I leave out the part where I want her in my bed. Now is not the time to say that.

"But—" she starts, and I shake my head to stop her. "Cat, I'm willing to go as slow as you need me to. We can date, do family stuff together, and eventually, when you're ready… you will be my wife."

"Wife!" she exclaims.

"Yes!" Cole screams, jumping up and down now.

Cat stands up and puts her hands on Cole's shoulders. "Hey, bud, since it's late, we're going to stay here tonight so why don't you head up to your room, and we'll talk more in the morning."

Cole looks alarmed, no doubt fearful that she's going to say no. The other day, I would have felt the same, but now after she told me she loved me and I claimed her in front of the whole stadium tonight, she's going to say yes. It's just going to take some convincing.

I fist-bump Cole. "Your room is ready for you. There's some clothes to sleep in, and I put a toothbrush in the bathroom for you."

He nods. "Good night, Holden. Good night, Mom."

He hugs his mom, and as soon as he's out of the room, she turns on me. "Holden Gray, what are you thinking? You should have talked to me about this first."

I grab her and move us to the couch so she's sitting on my lap. "I know that. Do you forgive me?"

"This is all just moving so fast."

"I know what it's like to share a home with you. Spending time with you and Cole, having dinner, hanging out, talking… I don't want to go back, Cat. I just want us to move forward. I love you, and you love me."

She puts her hand to my cheek. "I do love you, but I have an impressionable teenage son, and what's he going to think about his mom shacking up?"

I interrupt her. "We're not shacking up. You're going to be in your room and I'm going to be in my room—"

She looks at me with doubt. "Oh yeah, how long do you think that will last?"

"Until I wear you out and convince you to marry me."

She rears back. "What? You're serious about that?"

I put my hands on each side of her face and hold her close. "I know what my life is like without you in it, Cat. I need you like I need air to breathe. I want you to be my wife. I want to share every day with you and Cole. I want to hear about your days, be here when you need me. I want the good, the bad, all of it."

She wants to say yes. I can see all the emotions on her face, but she shakes her head. "This is crazy, Holden."

But she's here with me now, and I plan to take full advantage. "Stay here with me. I'll give you time to get used to me, we'll date, we'll do all the things… and when you're ready, you will be my wife."

She loops her arms around my neck. "Are you sure about this, Holden?"

I kiss her because I can't hold back anymore. She is the one for me, and I have no doubt about it. The kiss is heated, holding the promise of a future between us. I have to force myself to pull back. "Yeah, I'm sure. I love you."

"And you know I'm a package deal?"

"I love Cole," I tell her simply. "The kid is amazing, and I want to be the man he looks up to."

She shudders a breath. "Okay, we'll try this out."

I chuckle. "This is not a trial run, Cat. This is for me to shamelessly convince you to be mine."

"Okay."

I grip on to her waist. "Okay?"

She presses her breasts against my chest. "Convince me."

And I promise myself right now that I'm going to do just that.

# EPILOGUE
## CAT

## Three Months Later

"Any regrets?" I ask Holden as I look around the big space. Only one month ago, this was an empty warehouse. Now it's full of pitching lanes, hitting lanes, a weight lifting area, and a therapy room.

He wraps his arms around me. "Not one."

Since the day he retired as a professional baseball player and then turned down the coaching job, I've asked him the same question at least once a week. "You don't miss it at all?"

He kisses the top of my head. "Where is this coming from? I thought you'd be happy about me opening the training center."

I curl into him, pressing my cheek against his chest. How do I explain to him everything I'm feeling? Of course, I'm happy he put the training center here in Whiskey Run. And he's already proven that he's going to be busy. Heck, there are pro athletes that are scheduling time to come here and train with him, and I have no doubt he's going to make a success of this, but I still can't help but question him. I don't want him to ever resent me for this decision. "I am happy… I just want you to be happy."

He pulls back to look me in the face. "You make me happy."

I can't look at him and let him see all my insecurity. I was scared when I moved me and Cole into Holden's home and I kept thinking it would be temporary. For the first month, I held a part of my heart back, waiting for it all to fall apart, but Holden made it so easy to love him. He made it so easy for me to let my guard down and let him in completely. How could I not? Everything he did, he included me and Cole into the decision. He has shown up for everything. Practices, games, parent teacher conferences, he's brought me lunch more times than I can count, he asks me about my day and actually listens, and at night—well, at night, he brings me to his room and shows me how much he loves me in the best way.

"I'm just checking. There have been a lot of changes these last three months, and I wanted to make sure you're handling it all okay."

He nods. "Yeah, well, I wanted to talk to you about something."

I lean back and search his face and stutter, "Okay."

Is he finally going to ask me to marry him? These last three months have been wonderful, but I know if I could go to sleep next to him each night and then wake up next to him in the morning, it would be perfect. I even told him I should just talk to Cole about it, but Holden said no. He doesn't want us to share a room until we're married.

Now if only he'd ask me.

"So I've been thinking, and I know how my life could be even better."

Oh God, this is it. He's going to ask me. "How?"

He lets go of me and walks across the room, turning on the light to the therapy room. He gestures to the room. "I want you to work here."

I stumble on my feet even though I haven't even moved. "You want what?"

He holds his hands up. "I know you like your job, but I thought it would be perfect, if you wanted to, if you worked here as a therapist. We would get to see each other all day… we could build this together."

I rapidly blink, and I don't even try to hide my astonishment. "You want me to work here?"

He comes to me. "Are you okay? You're pale as a ghost. What is it? It was just a thought, forget I even asked."

He wraps his hands around my forearms. "No, I mean, maybe, we should talk about it. I thought you were asking me something else." I pull from his hold and walk across the space into the therapy room. I look around the room, at the state of the art equipment. I look everywhere but at him.

"Cat."

I force a lightness to my voice. "Yeah?"

"Stop. Look at me."

I grit my teeth. *You can do this, Cat. You can look at him without him knowing your heart is breaking in two.* I force a smile on my face. "I can see how it would be a good idea, but I need to think about it."

He's frowning at me as he comes toward me. *Oh God, if he touches me I'll never get through this*. I step to the side. "I should probably go get Cole."

He moves to step in front of me. "Dom is passing right by here, so I asked him to pick Cole up and drop him off."

"Oh," I say. That's another thing. I have gone from it just being me and Cole to a full-fledged family. Holden's brothers and sister have just brought us into their family like we belong here.

I pick up the magazine on the table and thumb through it. Determined to change the subject, I start to ramble. "I'm so glad to hear that Dom is going out on a date. I know you guys said that he's given up on dating and all that, but he's too good of a guy to be by himself. Do you know anything about the woman? I should ask Chrissy, she would probably know."

"Cat," he says, and when I don't look at him, he repeats my name. "Catherine. Look at me."

I lift my head and grip the magazine in my hand. "What is it?"

He comes toward me and doesn't stop until we're toe to toe. "What did you think I was going to ask you?"

I shrug. "It doesn't matter."

He puts his hands on my shoulders and holds me to him. "Talk to me, Cat. What did you think I was going to ask you?"

I struggle to get out of his grasp, but he doesn't let me. "Let's not do this, please. Cole will be here soon and—"

He releases me. "Stay here. I'll be right back."

He practically runs from the room, and I try to calm myself down. *I can do this. I can act like nothing has happened.*

When he comes back into the room, his face is flushed, but there is an excitement in his eyes. "I've wanted to do this for a while now, but I was waiting on you. I didn't want to pressure you, and I said I'd give you time but—" He sucks in a breath and drops to one knee in front of me. He holds out a ring box. "Cat, I love you more every day. The only thing that would make my life better is if you are my wife. And before I ask you, I want you to know that I talked to Cole about this around two months ago, and he gave me his blessing. Will you marry me, Cat?"

My mouth is hanging open. "But…"

He laughs. "There's no buts. We're meant to be together, Cat. Will you please marry me?"

With my heart racing, I throw caution to the wind. "Yes! Yes, I'll marry you."

He puts the ring on my finger and then he stands up, takes my face in his hands, and kisses me until I'm breathless. The sound of the front door opening has us pulling apart.

"Mom! Holden! Where are you?"

Holden is all smiles. "You want to tell him?"

I reach for my future husband and wrap my hand around his. "We'll both tell him." We walk out of the therapy room. "We're over here."

Cole is walking to us, and he is all smiles. The change in him these last few months has been a sight to see. He's so happy, I love seeing the smile on his face every day. I hold my hand up. "Cole, uh, Holden asked me if I'd marry him."

Cole starts running toward us. "You said yeah, didn't you, Mom? Tell me you said yes!"

Holden hugs me into his side, and I can't help but laugh as Cole is practically jumping with excitement. "I said yes!"

He pumps his hand in the air. "Yes! Now I'll have a dad and—"

He stops talking, and his eyes get really big. "I mean, not that you're my dad. I just mean…"

He stops all movement and is looking at Holden

like he expects him to freak out or something. Holden kisses me on the forehead and then releases me to go to Cole. He puts his hands on his shoulders. "Well, actually, when your mom and I get married, that's exactly what that means. Technically, I'll be your stepdad, but I thought about that, and maybe we—" He turns to look at me and gives me an apologetic look before turning back to my son. "I probably should have talked to your mom about this, but I had hoped that when your mom and I got married that your mom would let me adopt you so I could be your dad."

Cole is stunned. "You want to be my dad?"

Holden nods his head. "Yes, I would be honored to be your dad, Cole."

Cole bursts into tears, and so do I. I walk over to the two of them, and Holden wraps both of us up in his arms. His voice is thick with emotion. "I love you two… more than anything."

I squeeze him tighter. "I love you, too."

Cole buries his head into Holden's shoulder. "I love you, Holden."

A calm comes over me, and I soak up this feeling because I have my whole world in my arms and I feel like the luckiest woman in the world.

---

Want to read more about Dom and his date? Read
*Say Yes to the Fake Date*

Want to read Gabe and Chrissy's story? Read *Marry
Your Best Friend*

### *Whiskey Run*

Faithful - He's the hot, say-it-like-it-is cowboy, and he won't stop until he gets the woman he wants.

Captivated - She's a beautiful woman on the run... and I'm going to be the one to keep her.

Obsessed - She's loved him since high school and now he's back.

Seduced - He's a football player that falls in love with the small town girl.

Devoted - She's a plus size model and he's a small town mechanic.

### *Whiskey Run: Savage Ink*

Virile - He won't let her go until he puts his mark on her.

Torrid - He'll do anything to give her what she wants.

Rigid - If you love reading about emotionally wounded men and the women that help them overcome their past, then you'll love Dawson and Emily's story.

### *Whiskey Run: Cowboys Love Curves*

Obsessed Cowboy - She's the preacher's daughter and she's off limits.

### *Whiskey Run: Heroes*

Ransom - He's on a mission he can't lose.

Redeem - He's in love with his sister's best friend.

Submit - She's his fake wife but he wants to make it real.

Forbid - They have a secret romance but he's about to stake his claim.

### *Whiskey Run: Sugar*

One Night Love - Her one night stand wants more.

Rebound Love - She's falling for the rebound guy.

Second Chance Love - He is not a man to ignore... especially when he asks for a second chance.

Bad Boy Love - He's a bad boy that wants her good.

### *Whiskey Run: Guardians MC*

Protective Biker - She needs his protection and he'll give it to her. But he's going to need her heart in exchange.

Broken Biker - There's only one woman for him…

Relentless Biker - He won't stop until he has her back.

### Whiskey Men

Reluctant Husband - If you love reading about curvy women getting the hot guy, opposites attract, jealousy trope, marriage of convenience, and small-town romance, then you'll love Lucas and Isabella's story.

Something Real - If you love reading billionaire, single

father, age gap, boss/employee, and small-town romance, then you'll love Ford and Lilian's story.

Coming Home - If you love reading billionaire, ex-military, age gap, forced proximity, and small-town romance, then you'll love Hudson and Elle's story.

Forever Mine - If you love reading billionaire, age gap, second chance, and small-town romance, then you'll love Beau and Natalie's story.

Always Yours - If you love reading billionaire, friends to lovers, pregnancy, and small town romance, then you'll love Austin and Ally's story.

**Whiskey Men: Wounded Heroes**

Sweet Addiction - Curvy Single Mom and the Wounded Hero. Together in a brother's best friend romance.

Dark Obsession - Curvy Divorcee and the Wounded Hero. Together in an against all odds romance.

Unbreakable Bond - Curvy woman and the Wounded Hero. Together in an age gap, best friend's daughter romance.

Scarred Promises - A one night stand with the wounded hero.

# JOIN ME!

## JOIN MY NEWSLETTER

www.AuthorHopeFord.com/Subscribe

# BE A HOTTIE!

## JOIN HOPE'S HOTTIES ON FACEBOOK

www.FB.com/groups/hopeford

A place to talk about Hope Ford's books! Find out about new releases, giveaways, get exclusive content, see covers before anyone else and more!

# ABOUT THE AUTHOR

Hope Ford is a USA Today Bestselling author of Steamy, Sweet, Satisfying Romance.

She loves writing about small towns, swoony men, and curvy women that get their happily-ever-after.

To find me on Pinterest, Instagram, Facebook, Goodreads, and more:

www.AuthorHopeFord.com/follow-me

Want **FREE BOOKS?**
Go to www.authorhopeford.com/freebies